HORROR IN
SPACE

J. E. YOUNG

ILLUSTRATED BY COURTNEY HUDDLESTON

Story by J. E. Young

Pencils and inks by Courtney Huddleston

Coloring by Hi-Fi Design

Lettering by Marshall Dillon

Copyright © 2011 by Lerner Publishing Group, Inc.

Graphic Universe™ is a trademark and Twisted Journeys® is a registered trademark of Lerner Publishing Group, Inc.

Graphic Universe™
A division of Lerner Publishing Group, Inc.
241 First Avenue North
Minneapolis, MN 55401 U.S.A.

Website address: www.lernerbooks.com

Library of Congress Cataloging-in-Publication Data

Young, J. E.
        Horror in space / by J. E. Young ; illustrated by Courtney Huddleston.
            p.   cm. — (Twisted journeys)
        Summary: As the hero of this graphic novel, the reader is a space colonist who must rescue a spaceship from saboteurs and aliens by making choices that determine the outcome of the story.
        ISBN: 978-0-8225-9265-5 (lib. bdg. : alk. paper)
        1. Plot-your-own stories. 2. Graphic novels. [1. Graphic novels. 2. Interplanetary voyages—Fiction. 3. Extraterrestrial beings—Fiction. 4. Plot-your-own stories.] I. Huddleston, Courtney, ill. II. Title.
PZ7.7.Y68Ho 2011
741.5'973—dc22   2009032258

Manufactured in the United States of America
1 – DP – 12/31/10

ARE YOU READY FOR YOUR 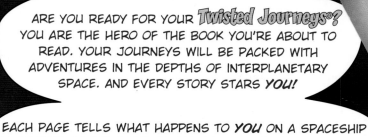? YOU ARE THE HERO OF THE BOOK YOU'RE ABOUT TO READ. YOUR JOURNEYS WILL BE PACKED WITH ADVENTURES IN THE DEPTHS OF INTERPLANETARY SPACE. AND EVERY STORY STARS *YOU!*

EACH PAGE TELLS WHAT HAPPENS TO *YOU* ON A SPACESHIP IN DANGER AT THE EDGE OF THE GALAXY. *YOUR* WORDS AND THOUGHTS ARE SHOWN IN THE *YELLOW BALLOONS.* AND *YOU* GET TO DECIDE WHAT HAPPENS NEXT. JUST FOLLOW THE NOTE AT THE BOTTOM OF EACH PAGE UNTIL YOU REACH A *Twisted Journeys*® PAGE. THEN MAKE THE CHOICE *YOU* LIKE BEST.

BUT BE CAREFUL... THE WRONG CHOICE COULD LEAVE YOU LOST IN SPACE *FOREVER!*

You dream of soaring through the universe on a vast, silvery ship. Space dust whispers past the hull, and comets with long, icy white tails soar by.

Special engines allow the ship to travel faster than light, but it will still take years to get to your destination—a star system named Cygnus 7.

Orbiting this star is your new home, a planet as beautiful as Earth and in need of colonists. That is what you and your family are: colonists. You can hardly wait to reach Cygnus 7, but wait you must. Lucky for you, you get to sleep, suspended in time, while the ship travels the vast distances of space.

"Captain. Wake up, please," you hear. The unexpected voice is that of a kid like yourself. Why is it calling you "captain"?

"Please wake up. We have an emergency."

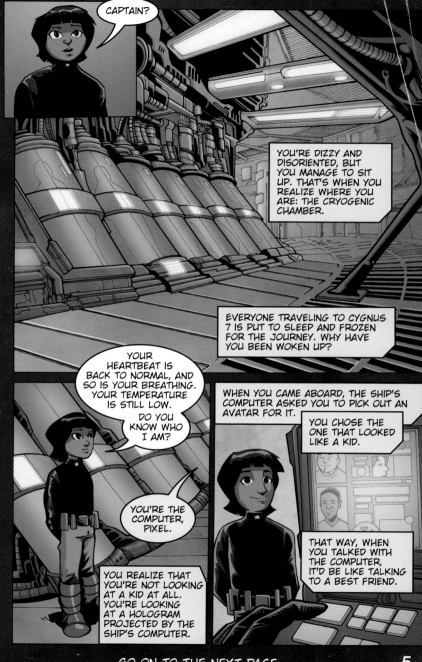

CAPTAIN?

YOU'RE DIZZY AND DISORIENTED, BUT YOU MANAGE TO SIT UP. THAT'S WHEN YOU REALIZE WHERE YOU ARE: THE CRYOGENIC CHAMBER.

EVERYONE TRAVELING TO CYGNUS 7 IS PUT TO SLEEP AND FROZEN FOR THE JOURNEY. WHY HAVE YOU BEEN WOKEN UP?

YOUR HEARTBEAT IS BACK TO NORMAL, AND SO IS YOUR BREATHING. YOUR TEMPERATURE IS STILL LOW.

DO YOU KNOW WHO I AM?

WHEN YOU CAME ABOARD, THE SHIP'S COMPUTER ASKED YOU TO PICK OUT AN AVATAR FOR IT.

YOU CHOSE THE ONE THAT LOOKED LIKE A KID.

YOU'RE THE COMPUTER, PIXEL.

YOU REALIZE THAT YOU'RE NOT LOOKING AT A KID AT ALL. YOU'RE LOOKING AT A HOLOGRAM PROJECTED BY THE SHIP'S COMPUTER.

THAT WAY, WHEN YOU TALKED WITH THE COMPUTER, IT'D BE LIKE TALKING TO A BEST FRIEND.

GO ON TO THE NEXT PAGE.

You climb out of your cryogenic chamber. When your feet hit the floor, you find that you're very wobbly, and also very hungry and scared. Why are you the only one the computer woke up?

"Pixel, what's going on?"

"We have an emergency, Captain," the hologram says very primly.

"Why are you calling me Captain? I'm not the captain."

"You are now," Pixel says grimly. "I've been trying to wake someone from the crew or passengers for weeks. You're the only one I could rouse. The rules are clear. The highest-ranking human awake is the captain."

GO ON TO THE NEXT PAGE.

The computer wants *you* to handle this problem?

WILL YOU . . .

. . . tell Pixel to put you back to sleep, use all its computing powers to solve the problem itself, and wake you when you reach Cygnus 7?
TURN TO PAGE 54.

. . . ask Pixel to tell you more while you head to the cafeteria for a snack?
TURN TO PAGE 50.

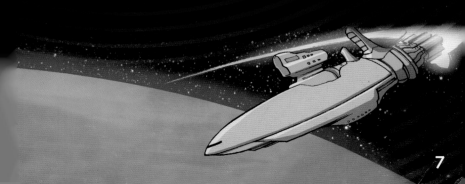

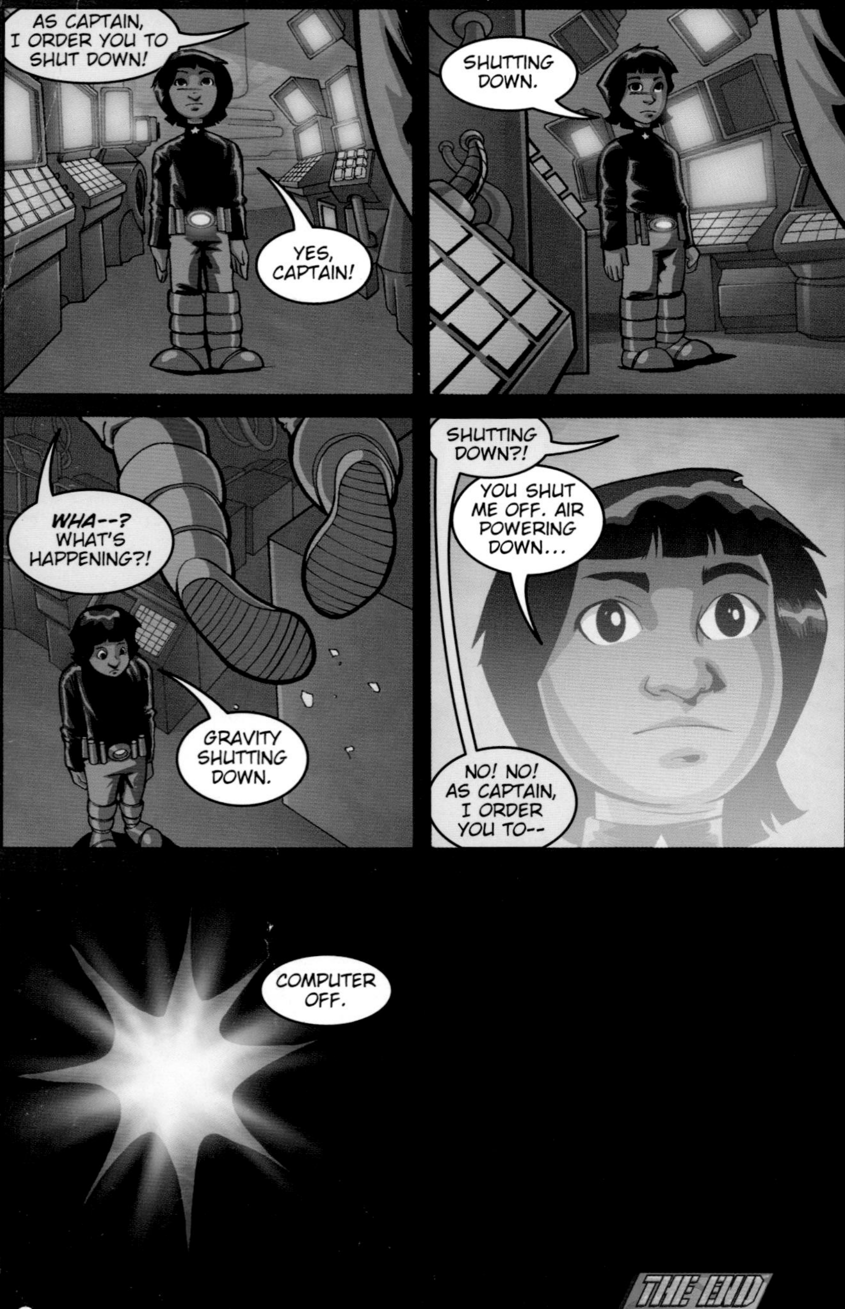
AS CAPTAIN, I ORDER YOU TO SHUT DOWN!
YES, CAPTAIN!
SHUTTING DOWN.
WHA--? WHAT'S HAPPENING?!
GRAVITY SHUTTING DOWN.
SHUTTING DOWN?!
YOU SHUT ME OFF. AIR POWERING DOWN...
NO! NO! AS CAPTAIN, I ORDER YOU TO--
COMPUTER OFF.
THE END

You gulp. But there's no real choice this time. The captain's right. Someone has to get those disks back. "I'll do what I can," you promise the captain, saluting. Beamer in hand, you head up to the storage room on the Cryo Level.

Your spaceboots sound loud as you creep toward the storage room door.

The door is open, and through it, you can see those precious disks still on the wall and Officer Nyche, busy at work at a control desk. His back is to you. You hold your breath, hoping he doesn't know you're there.

You step in, beamer raised and ready.

Officer Nyche spins around, a plasma gun in his hand!

"Stay right where you are," he says in a chilling voice. This man is not fooling around.

TURN TO PAGE 72.

9

Earth has never looked so amazing. You glide over the planet's oceans and continents, traveling at 2,500 miles per hour.

Soon you enter the upper atmosphere. The sky changes from violet to blue. Grabbing hold of Fido, you push a button. Out pops your first parachute. Captain Esme releases hers as well. The thickening atmosphere fills your chute and slows your descent to 120 miles per hour.

The next ten minutes are the most exciting of your life. The ground approaches. You and Esme release your second parachutes. The winds capture you, and you float toward an empty meadow.

"Happy landing," Pixel's voice says in your helmet, and your excitement melts into sadness. The ship and its computer will burn up in the atmosphere.

"Pixel! You said you'd find a way to be with me!"

"I'm downloading myself into a computer on Earth right now," Pixel says, "I'll see you again. I promise!"

TURN TO PAGE 109.

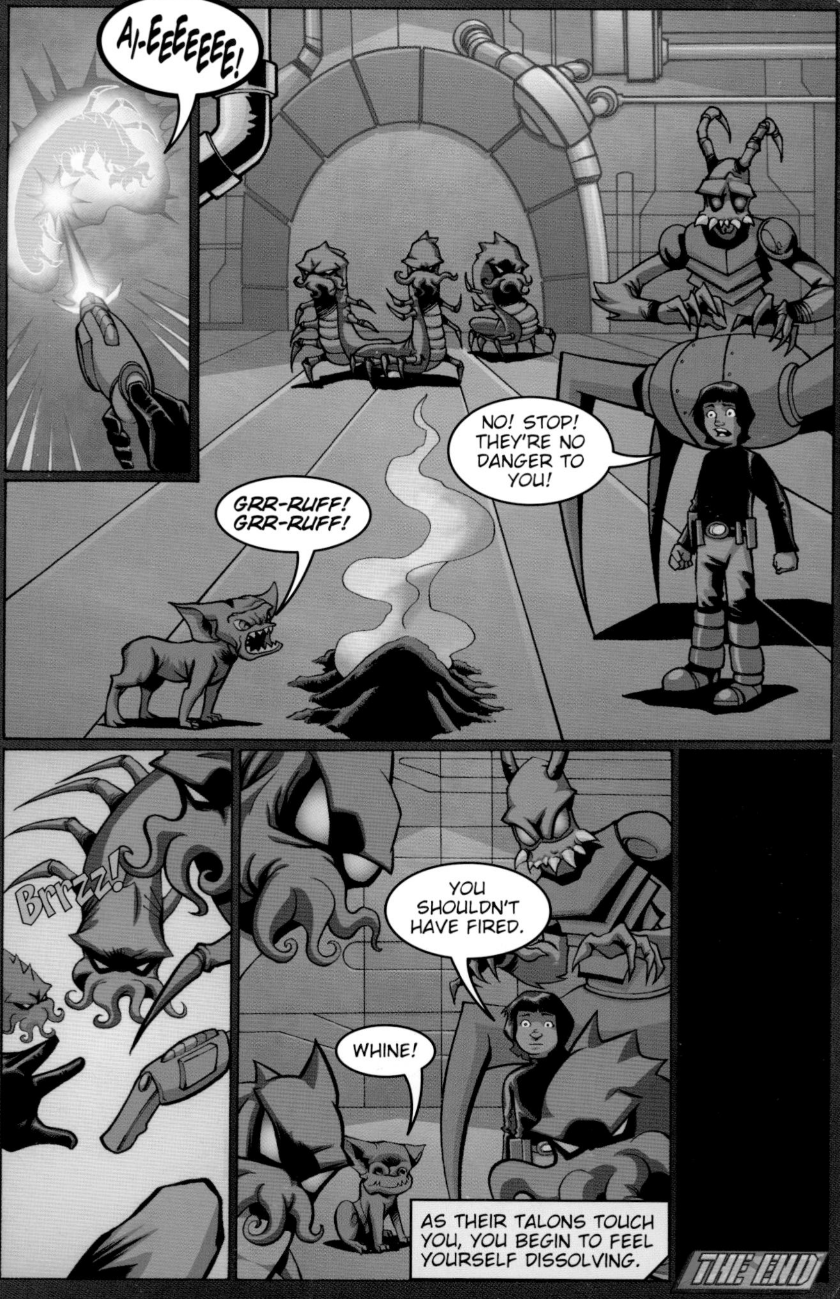
AI-EEEEEEE!
NO! STOP! THEY'RE NO DANGER TO YOU!
GRR-RUFF! GRR-RUFF!
BRRZZ!
YOU SHOULDN'T HAVE FIRED.
WHINE!
AS THEIR TALONS TOUCH YOU, YOU BEGIN TO FEEL YOURSELF DISSOLVING.
THE END

You pull the sandwich out of your pocket, aim, and toss it right into the cactus's mouth. The monster chomps down . . . then goes still. Thoughtfully, it chews on the sandwich, relishing it.

It no longer seems to notice you. Pixel opens the doors. You remove the beamer from your back pocket just in case, but the cactus is still busy enjoying the sandwich.

You make a dash for it and get out.

"This way," Pixel urges, leading you to a small computer room. The hologram points to a slot. "If you put the disk in there, I can get to work waking the person up."

You drop in the disk. "How long will this take?" you ask.

"About forty minutes," Pixel says.

Forty minutes. You're not sure you want to wait. You could use the time to check out the engine room.

It's probably better to wait where it's safe.
Then again, you do have a weapon.

WILL YOU . . .

. . . head down to the engine room?
TURN TO PAGE 55.

. . . wait in the computer room until the
security officer wakes up?
TURN TO PAGE 28.

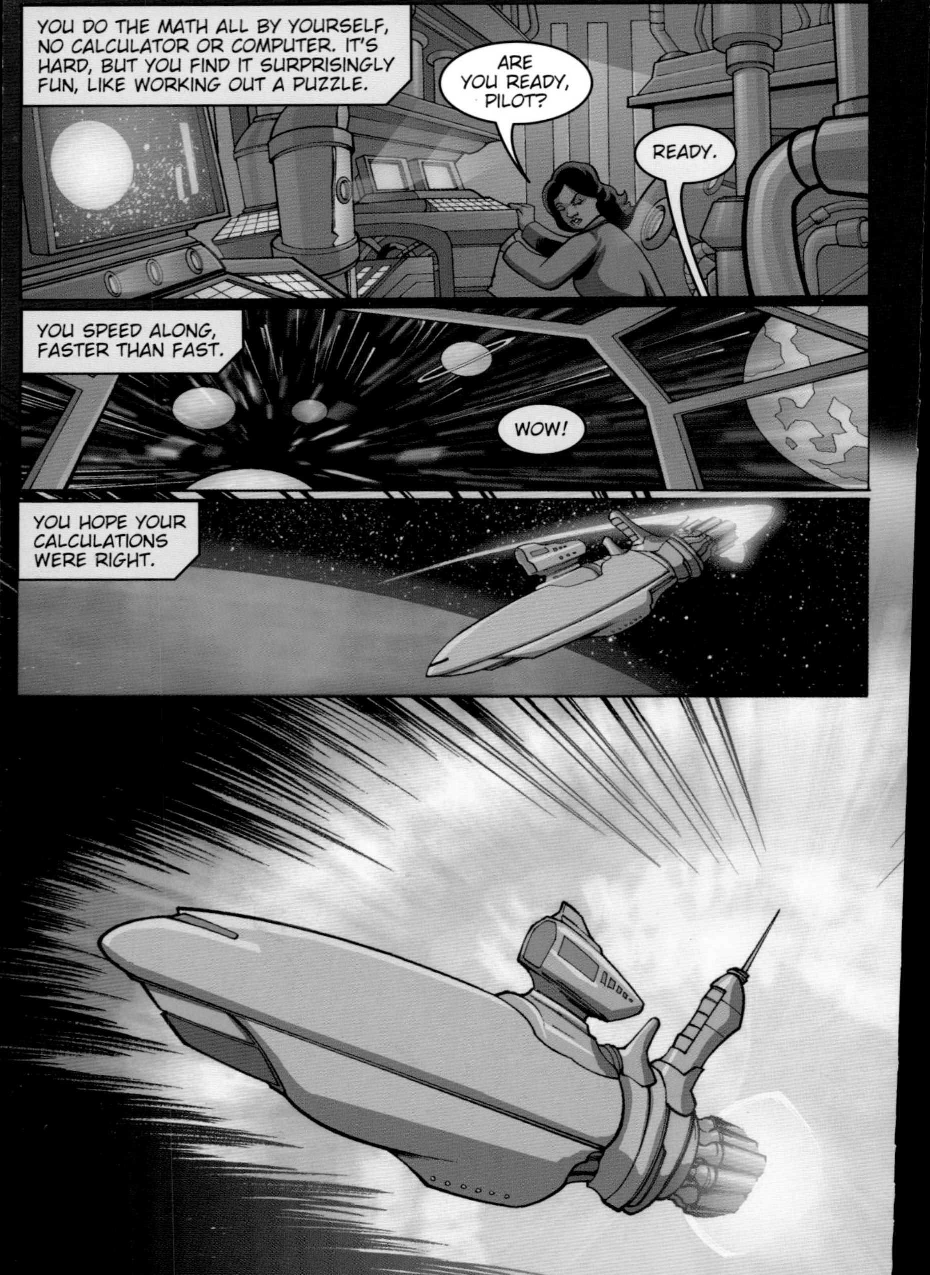
YOU DO THE MATH ALL BY YOURSELF, NO CALCULATOR OR COMPUTER. IT'S HARD, BUT YOU FIND IT SURPRISINGLY FUN, LIKE WORKING OUT A PUZZLE.
ARE YOU READY, PILOT?
READY.
YOU SPEED ALONG, FASTER THAN FAST.
WOW!
YOU HOPE YOUR CALCULATIONS WERE RIGHT.

Thanks to you—to your calculations and piloting—the ship escapes the supernova. Captain Esme is very impressed by and proud of you.

Once you are far enough away from danger, you go back down and gather up the disks. Pixel wakes everyone up. You are still in unfamiliar space and likely to stay that way, so the ship becomes your home. But that's all right with you. You've had the thrill of piloting it, and you don't ever want to leave it.

You study and train, and become the ship's pilot. Fido and Pixel are always there with you as you steer the ship toward new stars and planets, exploring a part of space that no human being has ever seen before.

THE END

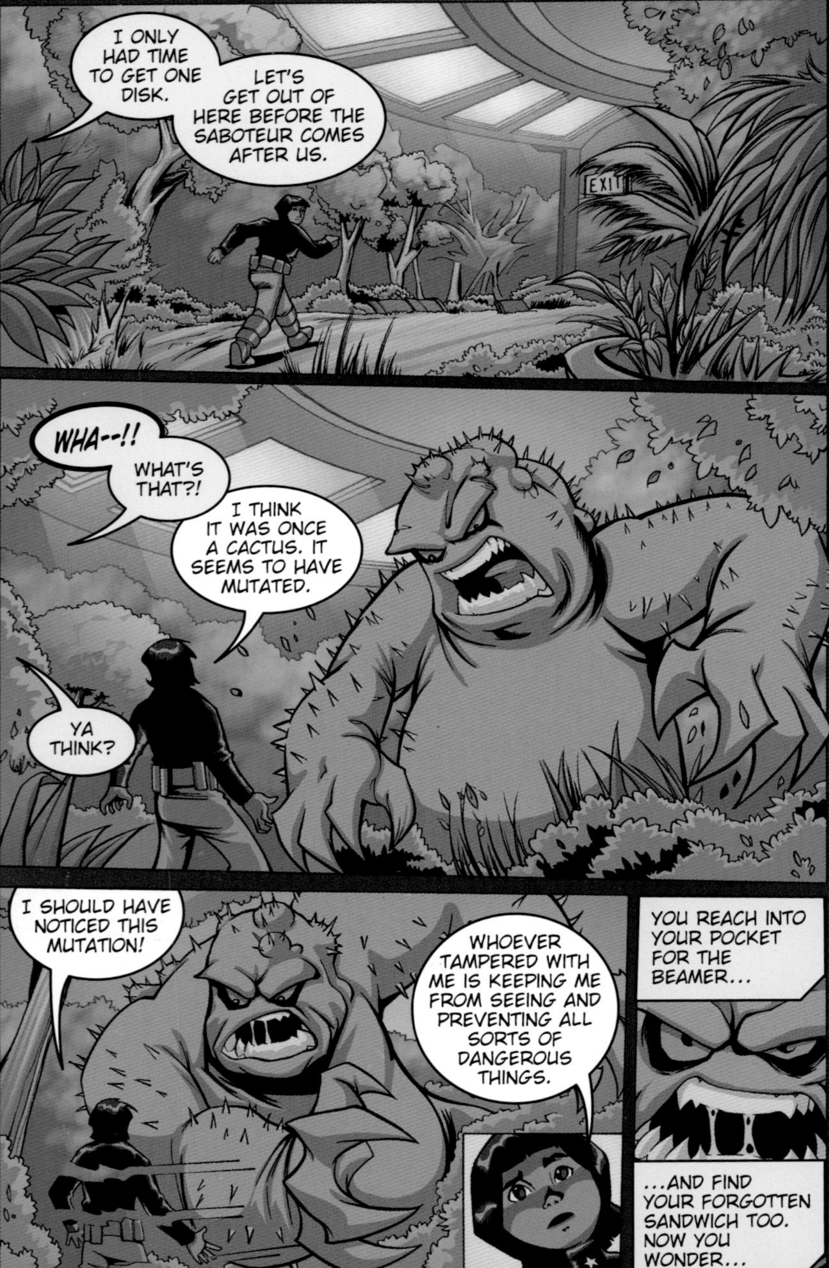
I ONLY HAD TIME TO GET ONE DISK.
LET'S GET OUT OF HERE BEFORE THE SABOTEUR COMES AFTER US.
EXIT
WHA--!!
WHAT'S THAT?!
I THINK IT WAS ONCE A CACTUS. IT SEEMS TO HAVE MUTATED.
YA THINK?
I SHOULD HAVE NOTICED THIS MUTATION!
WHOEVER TAMPERED WITH ME IS KEEPING ME FROM SEEING AND PREVENTING ALL SORTS OF DANGEROUS THINGS.
YOU REACH INTO YOUR POCKET FOR THE BEAMER...
...AND FIND YOUR FORGOTTEN SANDWICH TOO. NOW YOU WONDER...

TURN TO PAGE 44.

Captain Esme greets the alien. "Welcome aboard my ship," she says. "I'm sorry that one of my crew imprisoned you and is using your technology."

"I'm very sorry to have caused such trouble," the alien says.

"But why did he capture you rather than kill you?" the captain asks.

"I am part of my ship. If I die, it will have only one jump left in it—a leap home. Then it will stop working."

"Ah," she says. "I think I can override this man's connection to your ship and connect the ship to this bridge instead. If I do that, can you get us back on course?"

"Certainly."

Captain Esme turns to you. "You have done so much for us already, I hate to ask you to do more. But someone needs to stop Officer Nyche."

"I would like to help you do that," the alien offers.

Fido barks, also asking to come.

TURN TO PAGE 60.

The captain is appalled. "You brought us here just to gather up jewels?"

"Well, yes." Nyche is embarrassed. He looks at you. "One thing I'm wondering though. How did you get past my cactus? And what happened to the alien?"

"Fido took care of your cactus monster," you answer, "and I let the alien leave."

"WHAT?!" he yells. "If the alien and its ship are gone, then we're stuck out here, light-years off course."

Oh, no. What now?

You and the captain collect the disks and wake everyone up. It's decided that the ship will be your permanent home. Perhaps there are other spacefaring races nearby. And perhaps the riches of the black hole will be valuable to them.

In fact, there *are* others who travel this way. You and your ship become well known. In this part of space, there is no richer or more respected species than the strange humans who live near the quasar and mine its wealth.

18 *THE END*

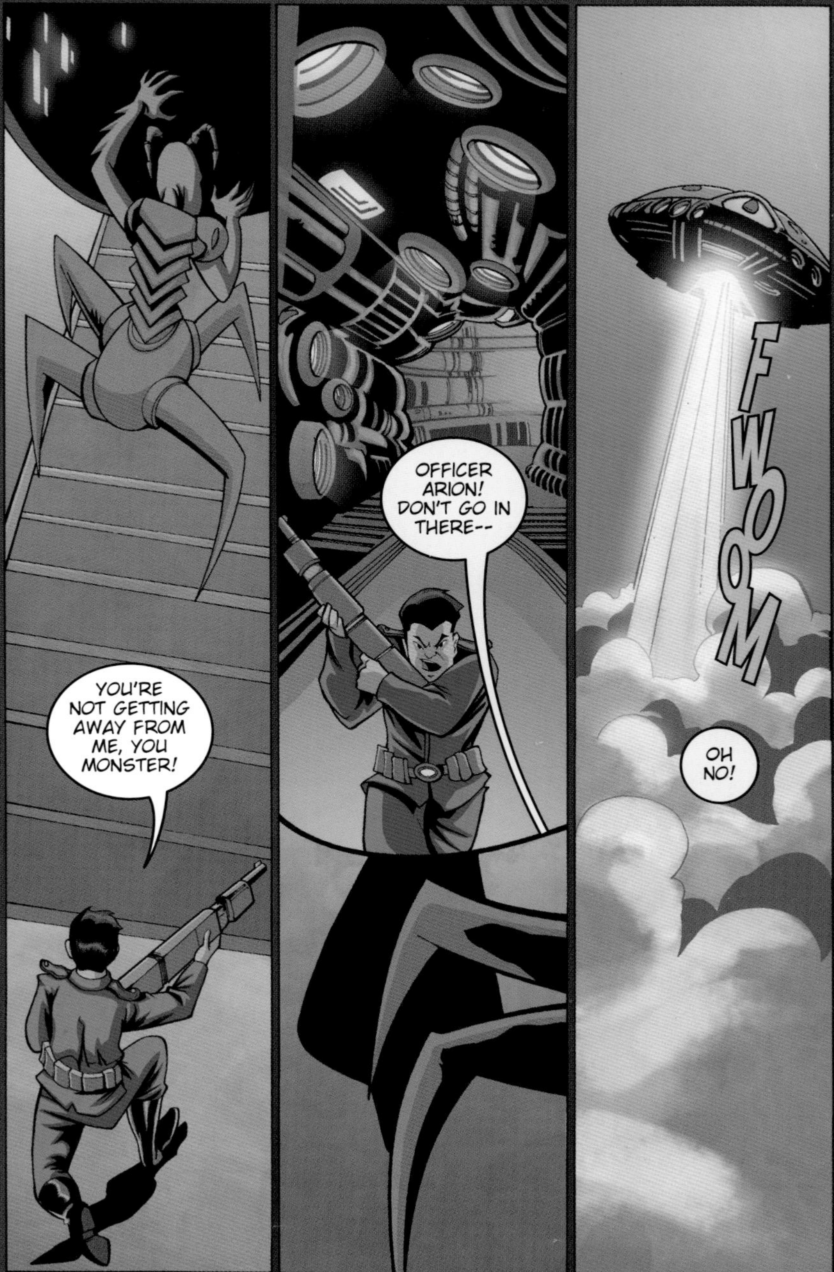
YOU'RE NOT GETTING AWAY FROM ME, YOU MONSTER!
OFFICER ARION! DON'T GO IN THERE--
FWOOM
OH NO!

TURN TO PAGE 82.

You follow Officer Arion down the corridor. He keeps his back to the wall, his rifle ready. You and Pixel stay close to the wall too.

"Ready?" Arion asks you as the storage room door comes in sight. It's wide open.

"Yes, sir," you say, getting a better grip on your beamer.

". . . NOW!"

Arion charges in. You're right on his heels. The man at the desk jumps up with fright and spins around. Clearly, he wasn't expecting you.

"Hands up!" Arion orders and then adds, with disgust, "Tech Officer Nyche! You traitor! What is this all about?"

"Riches," the man snaps back at the security officer. "I can mine the clouds around a black hole for wealth beyond imagination." Just then Officer Nyche notices you. His eyes widen. "You! I saw you go down the cargo hatch to the arboretum! How did you get past my cactus?"

"I gave it a sandwich," you say proudly. "It's probably still chewing on it."

20

TURN TO PAGE 84.

YOU'VE HAD TO MAKE A LOT OF HARD AND DIFFICULT DECISIONS TO REACH THIS PLACE.

COME BACK TO VISIT US! AND THANKS FOR THE SKIP TECHNOLOGY!

BUT YOU'VE GAINED SO MUCH!

YOU HAVE A NEW AND FAITHFUL PET...

GOOD DOG!

THE BEST FRIEND YOU EVER HAD...

YOU SAVED THE SHIP AND GAVE IT NEW TECHNOLOGY THAT WILL MAKE IT EASY FOR THE HUMAN RACE TO TRAVEL ACROSS THE UNIVERSE.

AND YOU GET A VERY SPECIAL OFFER FOR THE FUTURE.

WE COULD USE SOMEONE LIKE YOU ON BOARD. WOULD YOU LIKE TO JOIN THE CREW?

GO ON TO THE NEXT PAGE.

WILL YOU . . .

. . . become a colonist and develop
a new world?
TURN TO PAGE 88.

. . . become a crew member and travel
the universe?
TURN TO PAGE 88.

Following the alien through the new hole, you find yourself in the emergency dock. There, looming over you, is a fantastic ship. The hitchhiking aliens are already crawling up its long legs and passing straight inside.

Fido barks his strange bark and whines, not liking the idea of you leaving him. But you can't pass up this chance. You head up the ladder behind the alien. The inside of the ship is amazing.

You notice that Pixel is not aboard, but the hologram is no longer needed. The alien now speaks through its own machines.

"From what I gather, your ship cannot skip over the long distances between stars," it says.

"No," you say. "We have to spend years and years asleep while we travel."

"That is very sad. My ship can travel such distances in seconds. If you like, you could come with us as part of my crew."

What a tempting offer. And why not? The captain and Pixel can handle things here.

GO ON TO THE NEXT PAGE.

You're being offered the chance of a lifetime.

WILL YOU . . .

. . . say yes?
TURN TO PAGE 86.

. . . regrettably decline the alien's generous offer?
TURN TO PAGE 69.

You get the sandwich out of your pocket and hold it up for the mutated dog to see. It stops snarling and sniffs the air. Its head cocks one way and then the other with interest.

"Captain?" Pixel says, uncertain of what you have planned.

"Here you go, doggie!" You toss the sandwich, hoping to get the dog to chase after it. Amazingly, the animal leaps up way high and snaps hold of the sandwich before it has hardly left your hand. The dog lands and starts to chow down.

The sandwich is gone in a few bites, and you step back, worried that the dog might try to eat *you* now. You reach into your back pocket for your beamer.

"Yip! Yip!" the dog barks, wagging its tail and gazing up adoringly at you.

"Um . . . sit!" you command it, and it does. Pixel is amazed and impressed.

"It seems you've made a friend," the computer remarks.

"I think I'll call him Fido," you decide, patting the creature on the head. "Let's get out of here."

You and Pixel head into the arboretum, the side of the Bio Level that's filled with plants. Fido, yipping and barking happily, trots after you.

You're almost to the exit, when you see something else in your way.

GO ON TO THE NEXT PAGE.

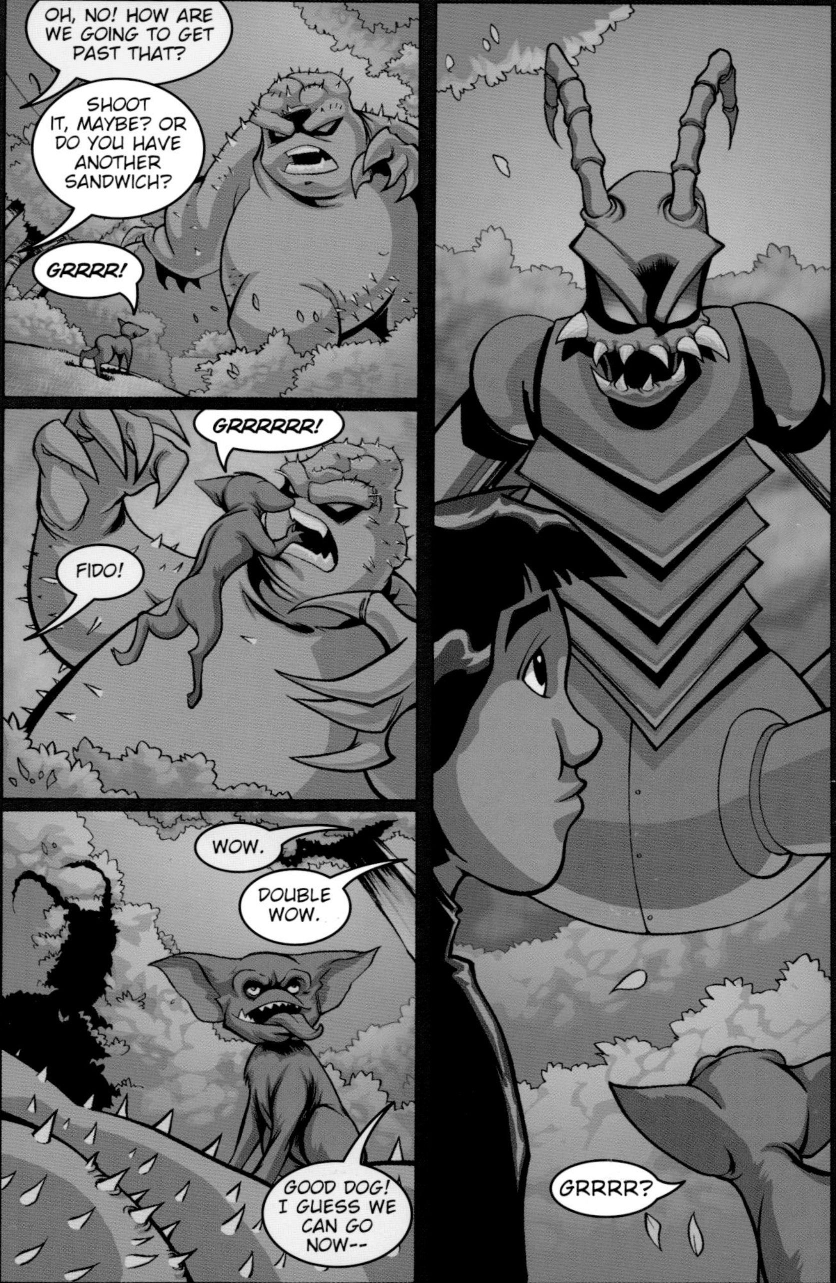
OH, NO! HOW ARE WE GOING TO GET PAST THAT?
SHOOT IT, MAYBE? OR DO YOU HAVE ANOTHER SANDWICH?
GRRRR!
GRRRRRR!
FIDO!
WOW.
DOUBLE WOW.
GOOD DOG! I GUESS WE CAN GO NOW--
GRRRR?

TURN TO PAGE 80.

You wait with Pixel. The forty minutes seem to take forever to pass.

"Can't you just use the security officer's information to wake up other people?" you ask the computer.

Pixel looks contrite. "No. I can learn some things, like how to play chess or how to express emotions. But I can't use information from one person in cryo to wake another. That takes guesswork. Only humans can do that."

"You make it sound like *we're* amazing," you remark.

"You are!" Pixel says enthusiastically. "You created me, didn't you? And this ship. And you're willing to travel for years just to see what's out here. That's very special."

You blush and are about to say something, when Pixel interrupts.

"Security Officer Arion is awake," the hologram informs you. "He wants to see you on the Cryo Level. He says, 'Watch out for the saboteur.'"

GO ON TO THE NEXT PAGE.

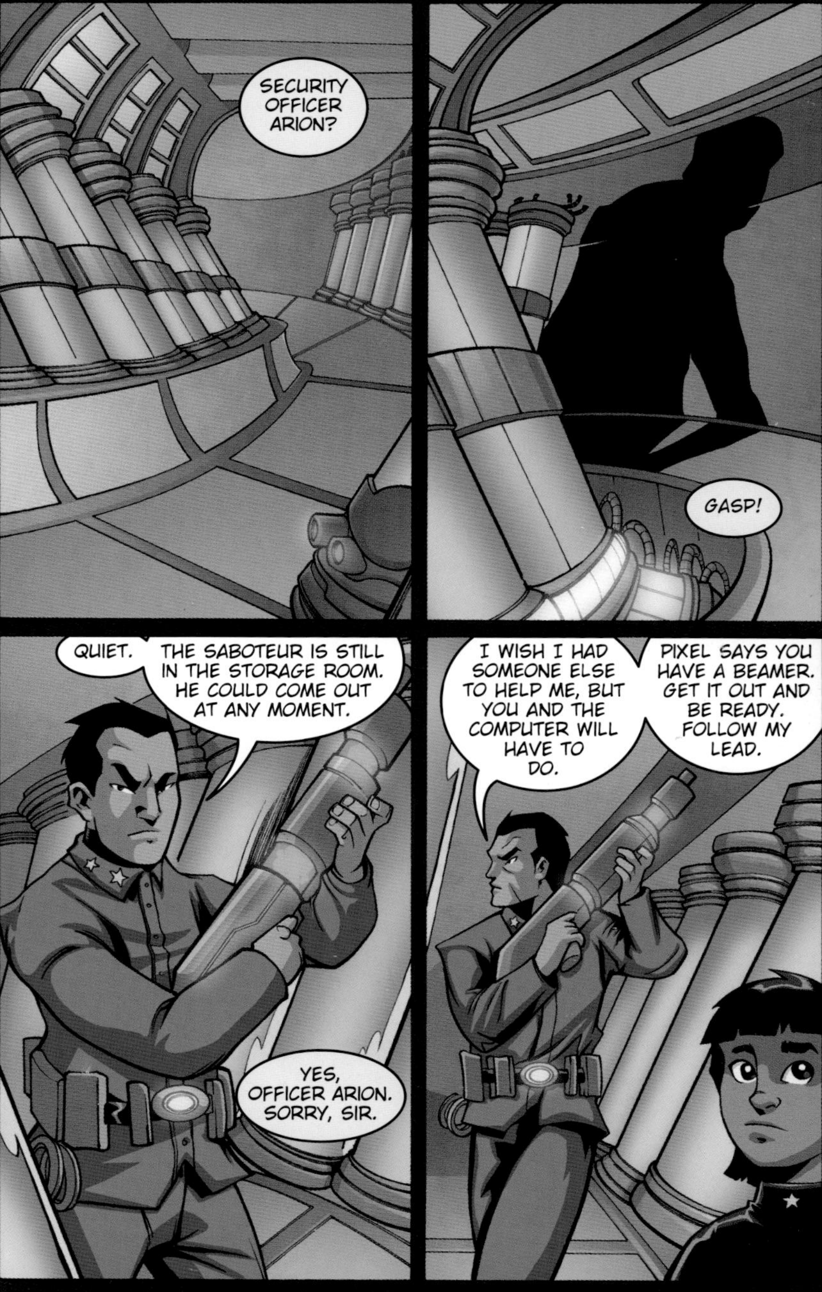
SECURITY OFFICER ARION?
GASP!
QUIET.
THE SABOTEUR IS STILL IN THE STORAGE ROOM. HE COULD COME OUT AT ANY MOMENT.
YES, OFFICER ARION. SORRY, SIR.
I WISH I HAD SOMEONE ELSE TO HELP ME, BUT YOU AND THE COMPUTER WILL HAVE TO DO.
PIXEL SAYS YOU HAVE A BEAMER. GET IT OUT AND BE READY. FOLLOW MY LEAD.

TURN TO PAGE 20.

You gaze up longingly at the ship as the aliens vanish inside, but you stay with Pixel. "I guess it's better to wait till the security officer wakes up," you say.

"Yes." Pixel is relieved. Then, suddenly, the hologram looks alarmed. "Captain!" it cries, pointing.

You spin. Framed in that hole in the wall is another alien. A very scary alien.

"I think that's the owner of the ship—" you start to say, reaching for the beamer.

Too late! The creature, protective of its ship, bounds through the hole and attacks!

You feel its mandibles latch around your neck and then . . . feel nothing ever again.

THE END

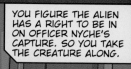

YOU FIGURE THE ALIEN HAS A RIGHT TO BE IN ON OFFICER NYCHE'S CAPTURE. SO YOU TAKE THE CREATURE ALONG.

YOUR SPACEBOOTS SOUND LOUD AS YOU CREEP TO THE STORAGE ROOM, BUT THE ALIEN MAKES NO SOUND AT ALL ON ITS SPIDERY LEGS.

STAY RIGHT WHERE YOU ARE--

URK!

WAIT! STOP!

"Wait for what?" The hologram of Pixel appears, speaking for the alien.

"We're here to capture him," you say. "Not kill him."

The alien's head tilts, perplexed. "He kidnapped me when I meant no harm. He held all your people captive in sleep as well. He took you off course and almost into a black hole. He is bad. You said so. Why let him live?"

"Because," you say slowly, "someone who makes wrong decisions should be allowed to put things right. He can't put them right if he's dead."

There is a long pause. Nyche hangs in the alien's grip, sweating and shaking with fear. Neither of you know what the alien will do.

"You are a most unusual species," the alien finally says, lowering Nyche to the ground.

"Y-you are a m-most unusual young person," Nyche agrees.

32   TURN TO PAGE 106.

One of the aliens is attacking you.
WILL YOU . . .

. . . shoot it?
TURN TO PAGE 11.

. . . hold off to show you are a friend?
TURN TO PAGE 62.

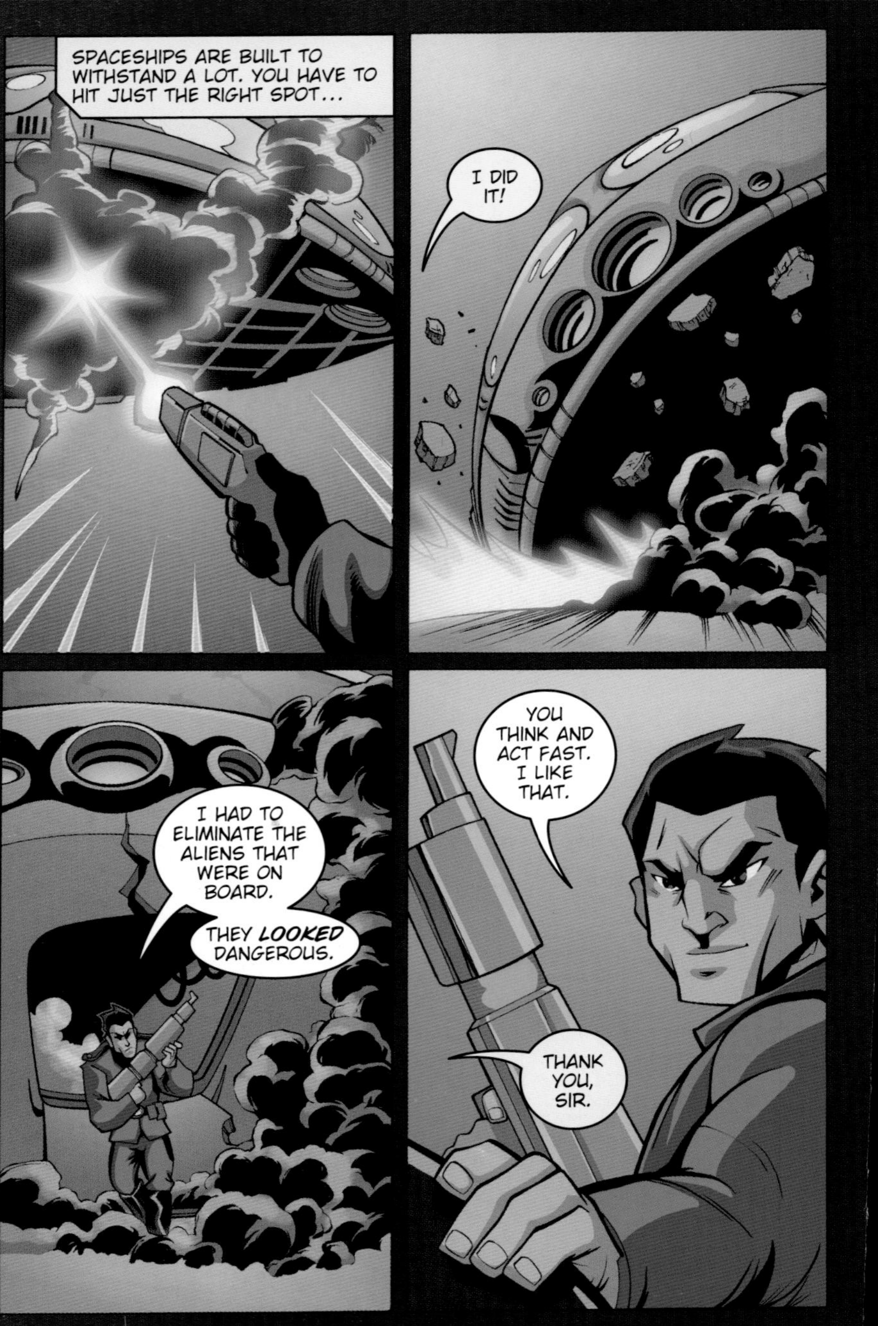
SPACESHIPS ARE BUILT TO WITHSTAND A LOT. YOU HAVE TO HIT JUST THE RIGHT SPOT...
I DID IT!
I HAD TO ELIMINATE THE ALIENS THAT WERE ON BOARD.
THEY *LOOKED* DANGEROUS.
YOU THINK AND ACT FAST. I LIKE THAT.
THANK YOU, SIR.

GO ON TO THE NEXT PAGE.

You and Arion go back to the storage room.

"Did you stop it?" Pixel asks.

"I brought down the ship," you say proudly, "and Officer Arion eliminated all the aliens aboard."

"What?" Officer Nyche cries out in horror. "If all the aliens are gone and their ship's been destroyed too, then there's no way for us to jump across light-years."

You feel your stomach turn over. "So we're never going to get to Cygnus 7?"

"Or back to any other area of space we know."

You wake the rest of the people on board. Captain Esme is understanding. She knows you had to do what you had to do.

The ship becomes your permanent home. Nyche is put to work with the biology team creating new plants and animals. Officer Arion,  impressed with your quick actions, teaches you all he knows. You grow up to be one of the security guards aboard ship, doing the dangerous jobs that need doing and keeping the ship and its people safe as you explore this strange new area of space.

THE END

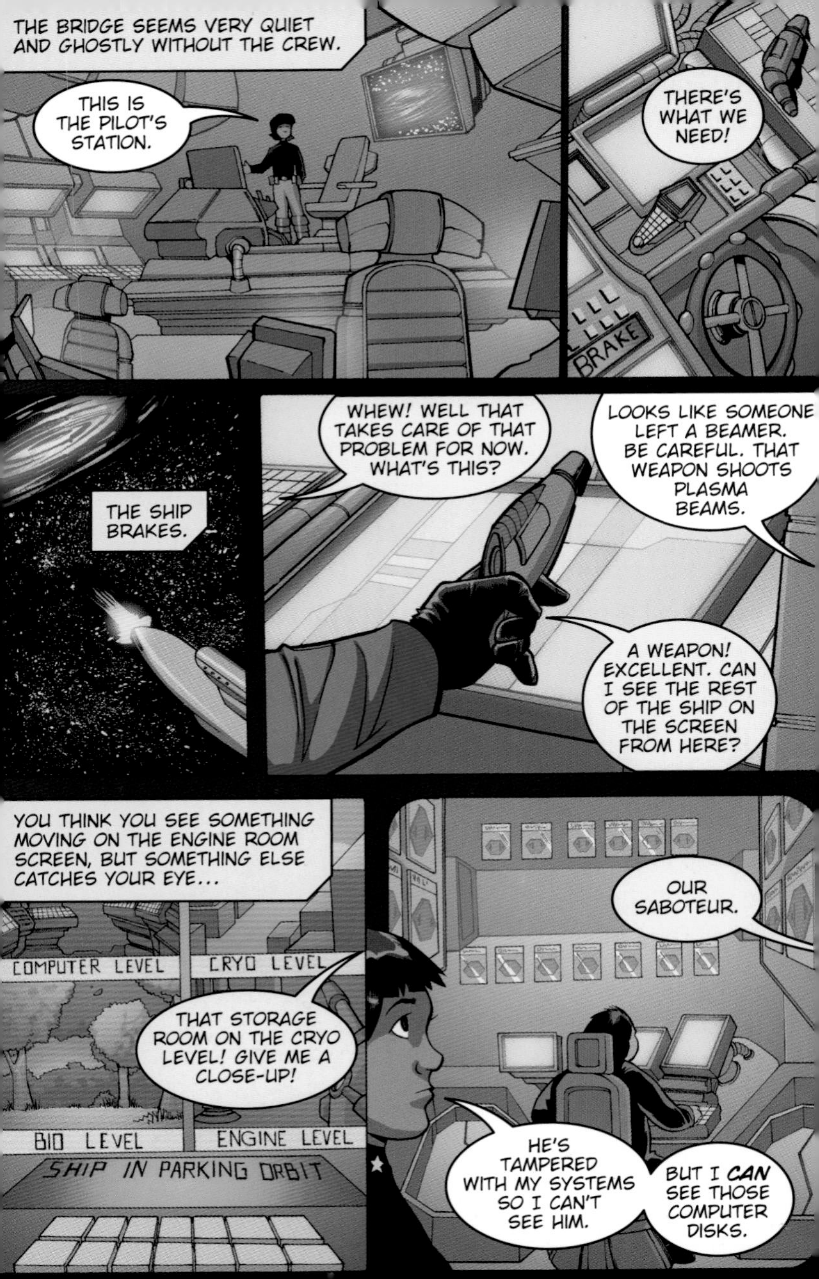
THE BRIDGE SEEMS VERY QUIET AND GHOSTLY WITHOUT THE CREW.
THIS IS THE PILOT'S STATION.
THERE'S WHAT WE NEED!
BRAKE
THE SHIP BRAKES.
WHEW! WELL THAT TAKES CARE OF THAT PROBLEM FOR NOW. WHAT'S THIS?
LOOKS LIKE SOMEONE LEFT A BEAMER. BE CAREFUL. THAT WEAPON SHOOTS PLASMA BEAMS.
A WEAPON! EXCELLENT. CAN I SEE THE REST OF THE SHIP ON THE SCREEN FROM HERE?
YOU THINK YOU SEE SOMETHING MOVING ON THE ENGINE ROOM SCREEN, BUT SOMETHING ELSE CATCHES YOUR EYE...
COMPUTER LEVEL
CRYO LEVEL
THAT STORAGE ROOM ON THE CRYO LEVEL! GIVE ME A CLOSE-UP!
BIO LEVEL
ENGINE LEVEL
SHIP IN PARKING ORBIT
OUR SABOTEUR.
HE'S TAMPERED WITH MY SYSTEMS SO I CAN'T SEE HIM.
BUT I CAN SEE THOSE COMPUTER DISKS.

"There's special medical information about each person telling me how to wake them up," Pixel goes on to explain. "I couldn't find any of it in my memory, none except for yours. It was as if it had been removed."

"So you think he took all the information on how to wake people up and downloaded it onto those disks?"

"Maybe. If you could get some of them," the computer adds, "maybe I could wake more people up."

You feel yourself go cold with fear at the suggestion. What if the saboteur catches you?

GO ON TO THE NEXT PAGE.

You need help, but you don't want to come face-to-face with this dangerous man.

WILL YOU . . .

. . . go down to the engine room instead and find out what you saw moving?
TURN TO PAGE 55.

. . . go after those disks?
TURN TO PAGE 100.

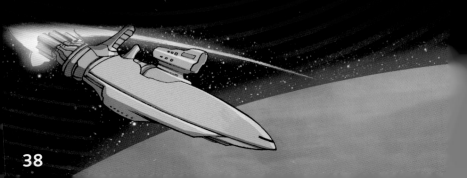

You take the vacuum shoot up to the Cryo Level. Your spaceboots sound loud as you creep toward the storage room door.

The door is open, and through it, you can see those precious disks, still on the wall, and Officer Nyche, busy at work at a control desk. His back is to you. You hold your breath, hoping he doesn't know you're there.

You step in, beamer raised and ready.

Officer Nyche spins around, a plasma gun in his hand!

"Stay right where you are," he says in a chilling voice. This man is not fooling around.

GO ON TO THE NEXT PAGE.

TWISTED JOURNEYS®

You've never used a beamer on anyone.

WILL YOU . . .

. . . fire on Nyche?
TURN TO PAGE 57.

. . . try to talk to Nyche?
TURN TO PAGE 93.

Forty minutes pass, and then Captain Esme appears on the monitor. "Pixel has brought me up to speed on all that's been happening," she says, "and all you've done. Given your youth and the danger, I hate to ask more of you, but I must. Our saboteur is Officer Nyche, a very clever and ambitious man. He found some alien technology that allowed him to jump this ship twenty light-years across space, into orbit around a black hole!"

Twenty light-years! Wow. That's a long distance, farther than the distance from Earth to Cygnus 7.

"In order to do this without alerting Pixel, he hacked the computer," she explains. "I'm on the bridge trying to get Pixel back to normal. Which is why . . ." Captain Esme stops and draws in a deep breath. "I need you to stop Officer Nyche and retrieve those disks."

TURN TO PAGE 9.

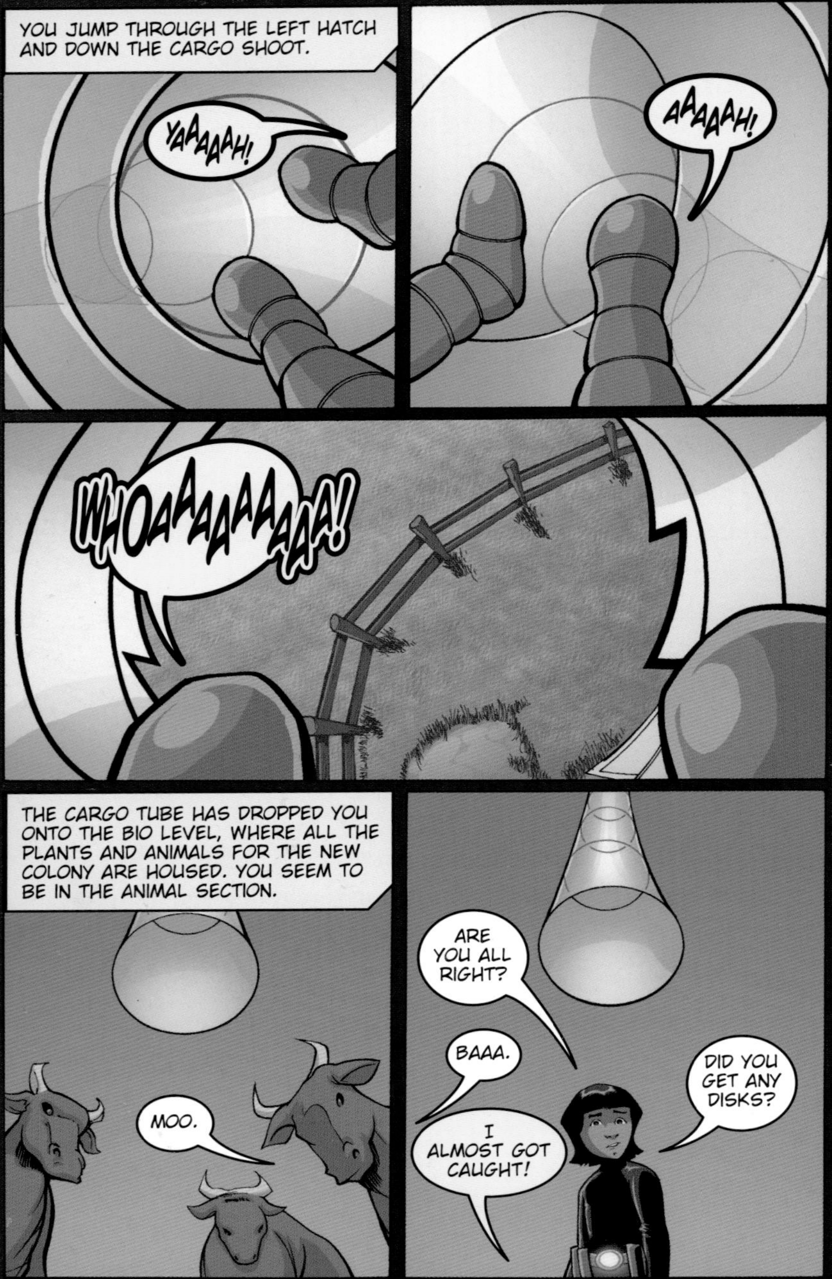
YOU JUMP THROUGH THE LEFT HATCH AND DOWN THE CARGO SHOOT.
YAAAAAH!
AAAAAH!
WHOAAAAAAAAAA!
THE CARGO TUBE HAS DROPPED YOU ONTO THE BIO LEVEL, WHERE ALL THE PLANTS AND ANIMALS FOR THE NEW COLONY ARE HOUSED. YOU SEEM TO BE IN THE ANIMAL SECTION.
MOO.
ARE YOU ALL RIGHT?
BAAA.
DID YOU GET ANY DISKS?
I ALMOST GOT CAUGHT!

TURN TO PAGE 63.

"I won't keep you if you want to get back to your own ship," you say to the alien. "But can you wait and speak with my captain?"

The alien seems worried.

"Fido and I won't let you be taken prisoner again," you promise. "The man who did that is bad. We almost fell into a black hole because of him."

"Yes," Pixel says for the alien. "We are not where we were when I came aboard this ship. This person must have connected your instruments to mine and used my ship's skip technology to jump us here. This is terrible. Of course I'll speak with your captain."

You head to a computer room and drop in the captain's disk. While you wait for the captain to wake up, you tell the alien about Cygnus 7 and the life you hope to have there.

Soon the captain is awake and asking you both to come to the bridge.

TURN TO PAGE 17.

43

WILL YOU . . .

. . . pull out the beamer and fire?
TURN TO PAGE 73.

. . . toss the sandwich into the
cactus monster's mouth?
TURN TO PAGE 12.

The pilot's screen tells you the ship's current speed, the speed the engines will give the ship, and the mass and gravitational pull of the planets.

Going around a planet is like grabbing hold of a tree trunk while on roller skates. If the tree is thin, you won't speed away very fast or very far. But if it's too big, it'll be hard to get around. It has to be just right to slingshot you.

There are so many numbers, and you don't want to try to work out the calculations yourself. What if you make a mistake?

"Pixel," you say, "Help!"

The answer appears on your screen, courtesy of Pixel.

GO ON TO THE NEXT PAGE.

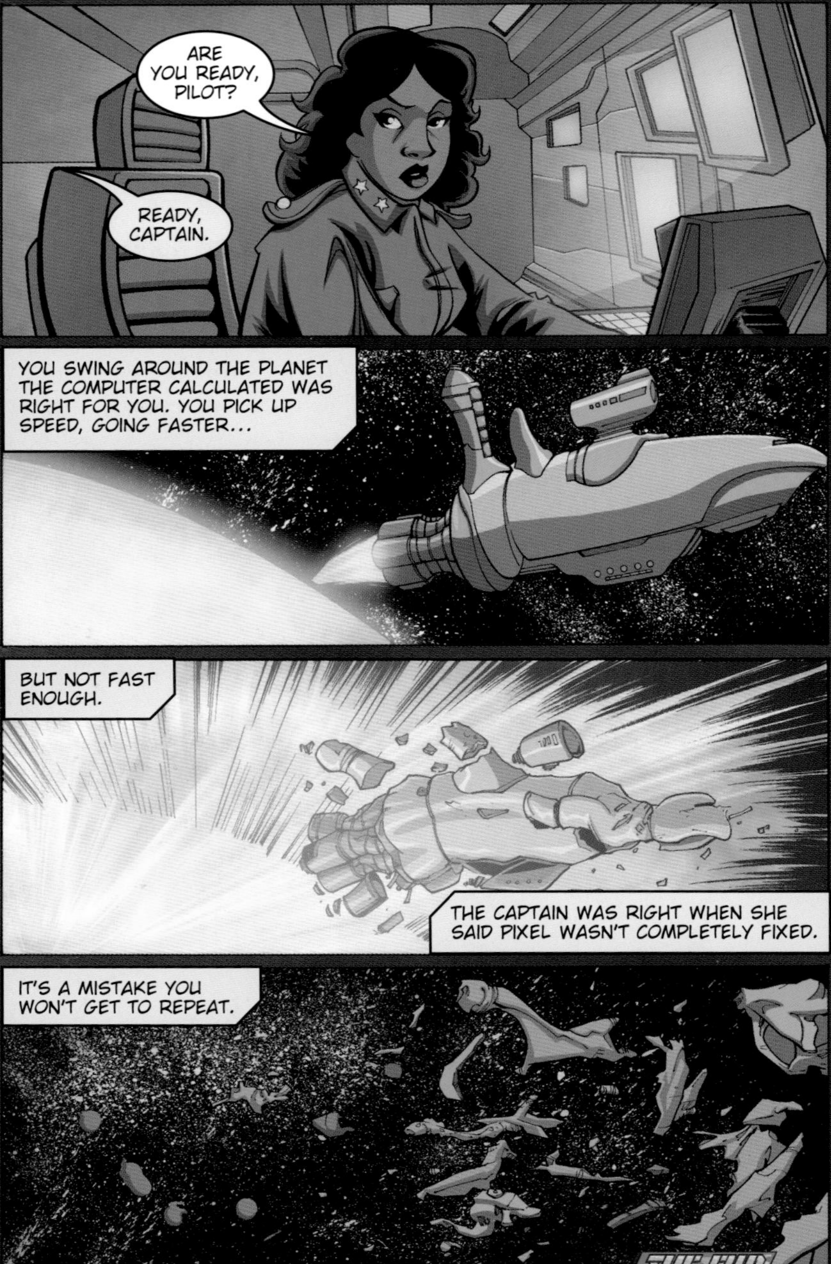

ARE YOU READY, PILOT?
READY, CAPTAIN.
YOU SWING AROUND THE PLANET THE COMPUTER CALCULATED WAS RIGHT FOR YOU. YOU PICK UP SPEED, GOING FASTER...
BUT NOT FAST ENOUGH.
THE CAPTAIN WAS RIGHT WHEN SHE SAID PIXEL WASN'T COMPLETELY FIXED.
IT'S A MISTAKE YOU WON'T GET TO REPEAT.
THE END

"Your ship is probably on the engine level," you say, opening the door. You step out into the corridor. The alien follows, moving Pixel with it like a puppet. "I'm sorry you had a bad time," you continue. "I promise to tell my people about you so that next time they'll be more welcoming."

"You're very kind." The hologram of Pixel says the words, but it is the alien who offers you a graceful bow.

"You're free to go back to your ship. You should use the ladder over there." You point it out. "Just go on down. Happy travels," you add.

"And to you, fellow traveler," it bids you as it heads toward the ladder. It leaves Pixel behind. The hologram blinks, as if waking up from a dream.

"That was strange," the computer says.

GO ON TO THE NEXT PAGE.

"We have to wake up the captain," you say, bringing out the disk. "Fido, come!"

You head down the corridor, the dog running after you. You find a computer room and slip the disk into a slot. Forty minutes later, you get a call from Captain Esme. She's on the bridge.

"Pixel has updated me on the situation. Our saboteur is Biology Officer Nyche, and he's damaged the computer," she tells you. "If not for you, we would have surely drifted right into the black hole!"

That makes you proud.

"I'm on the bridge trying to get the computer back to normal. I'm the only one who can do this. Which is why . . ." Captain Esme stops and draws in a deep breath. "I need you to deal with Officer Nyche. He must be stopped and those disks retrieved."

You gulp. The captain's right, of course. You're the only one who can stop Officer Nyche. But how to do it?

GO ON TO THE NEXT PAGE.

The captain wants you to deal with the saboteur.

WILL YOU . . .

. . . deal with him on your own?
TURN TO PAGE 39.

. . . take Fido down and face him?
TURN TO PAGE 58.

"Do you know why you can't wake anyone else up?" you ask Pixel as you get yourself a big, thick sandwich from the cafeteria.

"I think someone has tampered with me," Pixel admits.

"You mean, there's someone else awake? And they've hacked you?"

"It's the only explanation. That's why I need you," Pixel pleads. "I can't see what's wrong, but maybe you can. Please come up to my level and have a look at me."

The computer sounds so desperate, so embarrassed to be asking for help, that you feel sorry for it.

You take another bite of your sandwich, then wrap it up and stuff it away in your pocket. You head to the elevator, but Pixel cuts in front of you.

"Don't take the elevator!" the hologram warns.

"Why not?"

"I can't remember," Pixel says, frustrated. "There's a reason, but I think it's been erased from my memory."

"How should I go up then?"

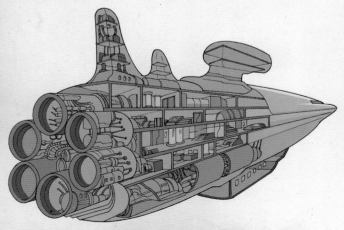

GO ON TO THE NEXT PAGE.

THE VACUUM TUBE IS FOR SENDING THINGS UP AND DOWN BETWEEN THE LEVELS. IT'S NOT SUPPOSED TO BE FOR PEOPLE, BUT TRAVELING IN IT MIGHT BE FUN.

USE THE VACUUM TUBE.

I'LL SEND YOU UP. READY?

SUDDENLY YOU'RE PULLED RIGHT UP TO ANOTHER LEVEL OF THE SHIP.

BLACK HOLE
10 hrs 14 mins

THAT WAS AWESOME!

WELCOME TO ME.

YOU FEEL A POWERFUL SUCTION, LIKE BEING IN A VACUUM CLEANER.

GO ON TO THE NEXT PAGE.

Only faint hums and dings indicate that there is a great machine at work. You are very aware at that moment that Pixel is maintaining everything on the ship: the temperature and atmosphere and artificial gravity, the lights and plumbing. Pixel is doing everything from driving the ship to keeping the sleeping passengers alive.

Pixel *is* the ship.

"This is amazing," you blurt out. "You're amazing."

Pixel blushes. "Do you really think so, Captain?"

"I sure do," you say, gazing up at the monitors. That's when you freeze. "We're on the wrong heading!"

This is an understatement. The ship is on its way to a black hole! Like a soap bubble swirling toward a drain, if you don't stop it, it'll be pulled right in!

"How do I shut you down?" you ask the computer.

"As captain, order me to shut down," Pixel answers dutifully.

GO ON TO THE NEXT PAGE.

In ten hours and twelve minutes, this ship
will be sucked into a black hole.

WILL YOU . . .

. . . order the computer to shut down?
TURN TO PAGE 8.

. . . head for the bridge to see if there's
another way to save the ship?
TURN TO PAGE 36.

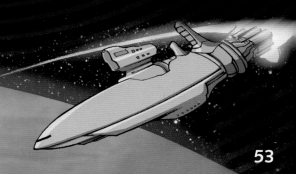

"I can't help you, Pixel," you say. "Put me back to sleep and work it out yourself."

"Yes, Captain," Pixel says, saluting you. The computer isn't happy, but since you are the captain, it will obey.

You lie back again on the pallet, and Pixel lowers the canopy. The air is cool on your skin, slowly lowering your body temperature.

A quiet and dreamy darkness envelops you.

Pixel puts all its computing power into trying to wake up someone else. Unfortunately, the ship is off course, and with Pixel focused on this new goal, it doesn't realize this. Not even when the ship reaches the event horizon—the edge—of a black hole.

No one on board this ship will ever wake up. You all will sleep forever. You fall eternally and without time, into the dark, dense center of the black hole, from which not even light can escape.

THE END

THE ENGINE ROOM IS AN AMAZING PLACE, VIBRATING WITH ENERGY AND ACTIVITY.

I'M SURE I SAW SOMETHING MOVING AROUND DOWN HERE. WAIT. WHAT'S THAT?

WHAT MADE THIS?

WHAT ARE THEY DOING?

TEMPORARILY DISRUPTING THE BOND BETWEEN ATOMS SO THEY CAN PASS THROUGH SOLID MATTER.

CLIK! CLIK, CLIK, CHRRRIP!

GO ON TO THE NEXT PAGE.

You have no idea if these aliens are a threat.

WILL YOU . . .

. . . fire the beamer?
TURN TO PAGE 89.

. . . tell the aliens that you mean them no harm?
TURN TO PAGE 66.

You fire!

"I'm sorry I had to do that," you say. It's too late, however. Officer Nyche has collapsed unconscious over the control panel. You collect all the disks, and with Captain Esme, you wake everyone on board the ship.

"Nyche connected us to the alien ship," Captain Esme explains to you later on, "and used it to jump our ship across light-years to this place. But now the alien ship is gone."

. . . which means the ship is stuck in this part of space. Pixel, however, has learned about alien languages from his connection with the visitor. Studying with Pixel, you become a translator. You and the other colonists make a new life for yourselves as explorers, and you are the one who communicates and negotiates with all the new species the ship encounters. You introduce the human race to the universe.

THE END

WITH A PLAN IN MIND, YOU HEAD UP TO THE CRYO LEVEL.

QUIET, FIDO. WE DON'T WANT TO ALERT HIM.

STAY RIGHT WHERE YOU ARE!

WAIT! THAT'S *MY* DOG CREATURE! HOW DID YOU--?

FIDO! ATTACK!

GRRRR!

CALL IT OFF! CALL IT OFF! I SURRENDER!

GOOD DOG!

Captain Esme arrives soon after. Officer Nyche is put into cuffs.

"It's a good thing you decided to wake me," she tells you. "I was able to fix the computer and get things back to normal."

That's a relief to hear. Now it's time to talk with Officer Nyche.

"I'm the biology expert," Nyche explains. "When the alien appeared on our ship, the computer woke me to deal with it. I realized right away that I could put its advanced technology to use. I created the cactus monster to keep it trapped. Then I hooked our computer into the alien ship and used it to jump us here, near the black hole."

"But why near a black hole?" Captain Esme asks.

"That isn't just any black hole," Nyche points out, "It's a supermassive black hole surrounded by a dusty cloud: a quasar. They produce rubies and sapphires."

TURN TO PAGE 18.

Taking both might make it hard
to sneak up on Nyche.

WILL YOU . . .

. . . take Fido and leave the alien?
TURN TO PAGE 65.

. . . take the alien and leave Fido?
TURN TO PAGE 31.

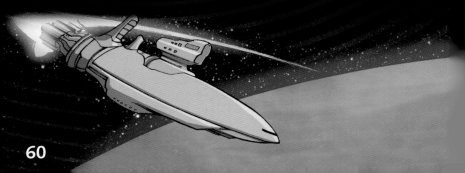

With your alien friends, you travel the universe, visiting other star systems and other worlds, seeing wonders no human has ever seen before, and having all kinds of adventures.

Now and then, you think about the ship, about Pixel and Fido and everyone you left behind. You sometimes wonder what happened to them and what your life would have been like if you'd gone to Cygnus 7. Maybe someday you'll find your way there.

Your days, however, are too busy and filled with new wonders for you to think about such things for long.

You are a star traveler, and the whole universe is your home.

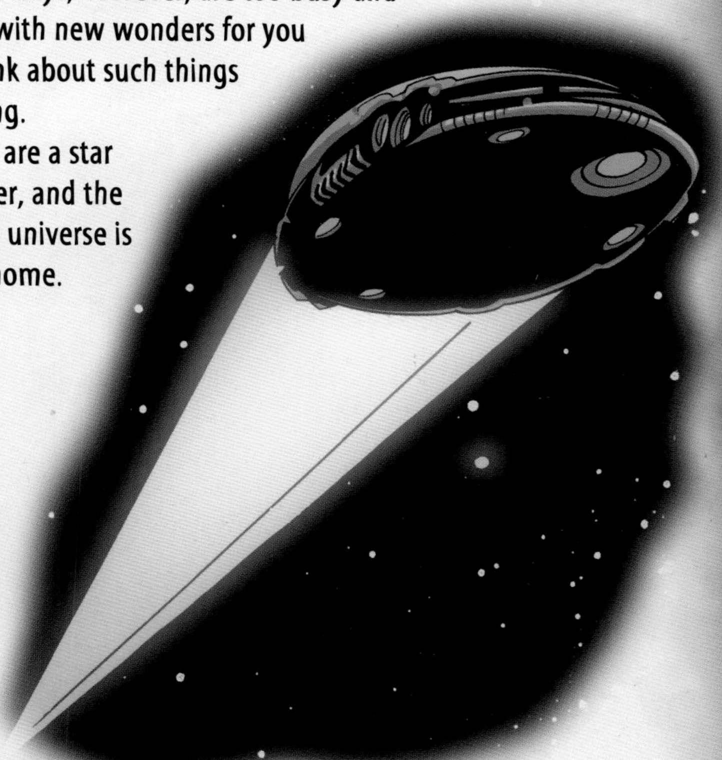

THE END

You're scared, but you don't shoot. Then the weird worm leaps at you. Fido barks in alarm.

"Klk! Klk!" The Spider Alien makes loud clicking noises.

To your amazement, the wormlike creature passes right through you and lands on the other side. You're unharmed.

"I'm sorry!" Pixel says, and the Spider Alien lifts its odd hands. "I was explaining my kidnapping, and they thought you were to blame. I shouted at them that you are a friend. Thank you for not shooting."

Whew!

"What are they," you demand, "and what have they done to the wall?"

"Their ship broke down, and I rescued them," the alien explains. "They are able to dissolve the bonds that hold atoms together, either temporarily or permanently. They only melted this hole so I can return to my ship. It is locked in there." The alien points to the other wall.

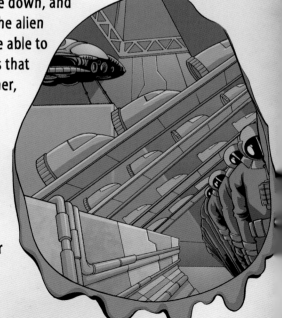

TURN TO PAGE 23.

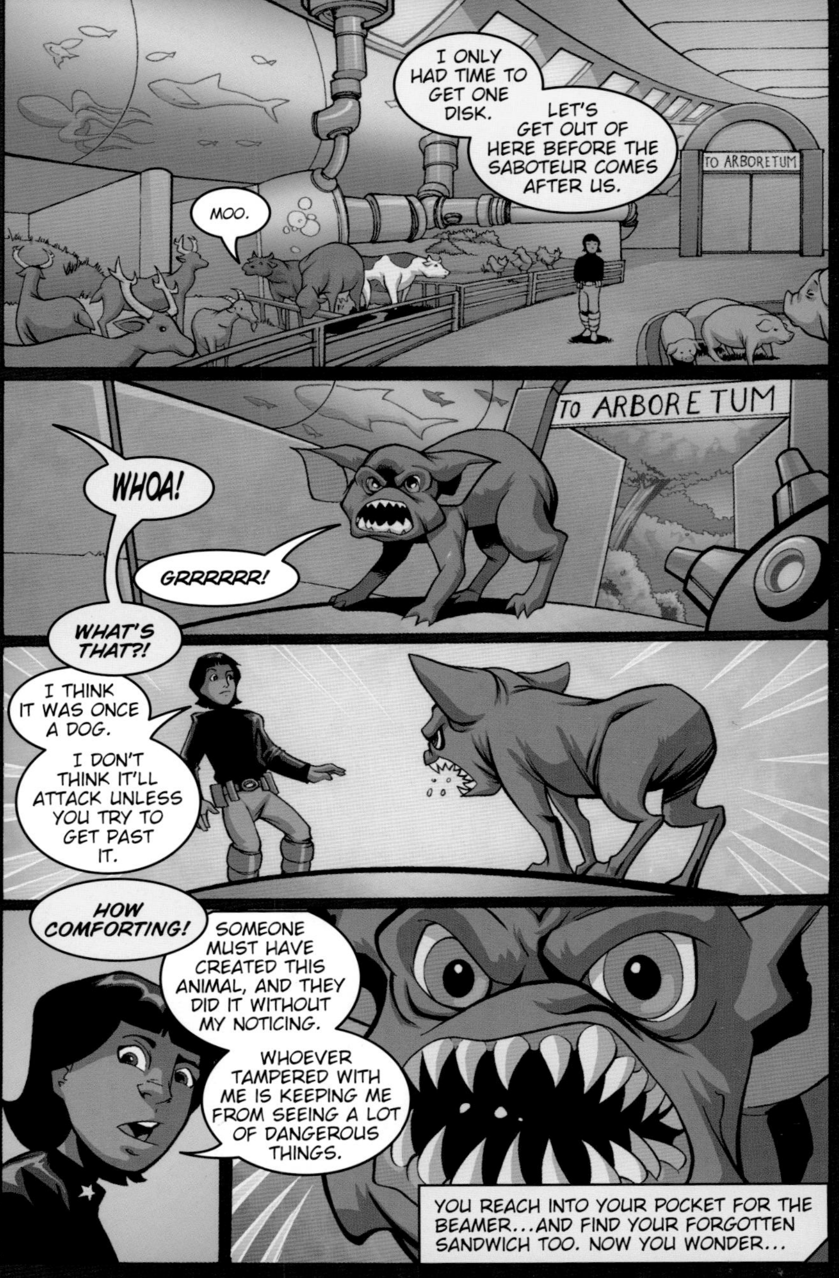
I ONLY HAD TIME TO GET ONE DISK.
LET'S GET OUT OF HERE BEFORE THE SABOTEUR COMES AFTER US.
TO ARBORETUM
MOO.
TO ARBORETUM
WHOA!
GRRRRRR!
WHAT'S THAT?!
I THINK IT WAS ONCE A DOG.
I DON'T THINK IT'LL ATTACK UNLESS YOU TRY TO GET PAST IT.
HOW COMFORTING!
SOMEONE MUST HAVE CREATED THIS ANIMAL, AND THEY DID IT WITHOUT MY NOTICING.
WHOEVER TAMPERED WITH ME IS KEEPING ME FROM SEEING A LOT OF DANGEROUS THINGS.
YOU REACH INTO YOUR POCKET FOR THE BEAMER...AND FIND YOUR FORGOTTEN SANDWICH TOO. NOW YOU WONDER...

GO ON TO THE NEXT PAGE.

WILL YOU . . .

. . . get out the beamer and fire?
TURN TO PAGE 105.

. . . get out the sandwich and toss it to the dog?
TURN TO PAGE 25.

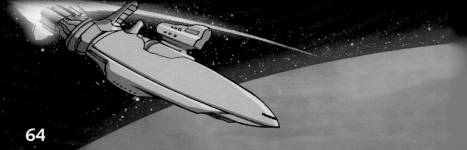

You thank the alien for the offer but explain that it's probably better if you and Fido handle this.

"Be careful," Captain Esme warns.

"We will be," you promise and head down to the Cryo Level.

Your spaceboots sound loud as you creep toward the storage room door, which is open. Fido growls, and you hush him. You can see those precious disks still on the wall and Officer Nyche busy at work at a control desk.

"Get ready, Fido," you warn, drawing your beamer.

Officer Nyche spins around, aiming a plasma gun at you. "Stay right where you are—" he starts to say. His eyes go wide as he sees Fido.

"Fido!" you shout. "Attack!"

TURN TO PAGE 106.

The aliens look startled, but not menacing, and you're more curious about them than frightened.

"I mean you no harm," you say, lifting your empty hands. Cautiously, the aliens creep forward.

"Careful," Pixel warns. "Don't let them touch you."

You nod and wait. The aliens don't touch you. Instead, they rise up on their tails and wave their tentacle mouths your way. You feel a slight electrical buzz around you, as if they are doing a scan of your body. Their glowing eyes gaze at you with interest.

"What are you doing on my ship?" you ask them.

They take a moment to exchange glances and touch one another's tentacles as if communicating. Then one jerks its head toward the wall.

GO ON TO THE NEXT PAGE.

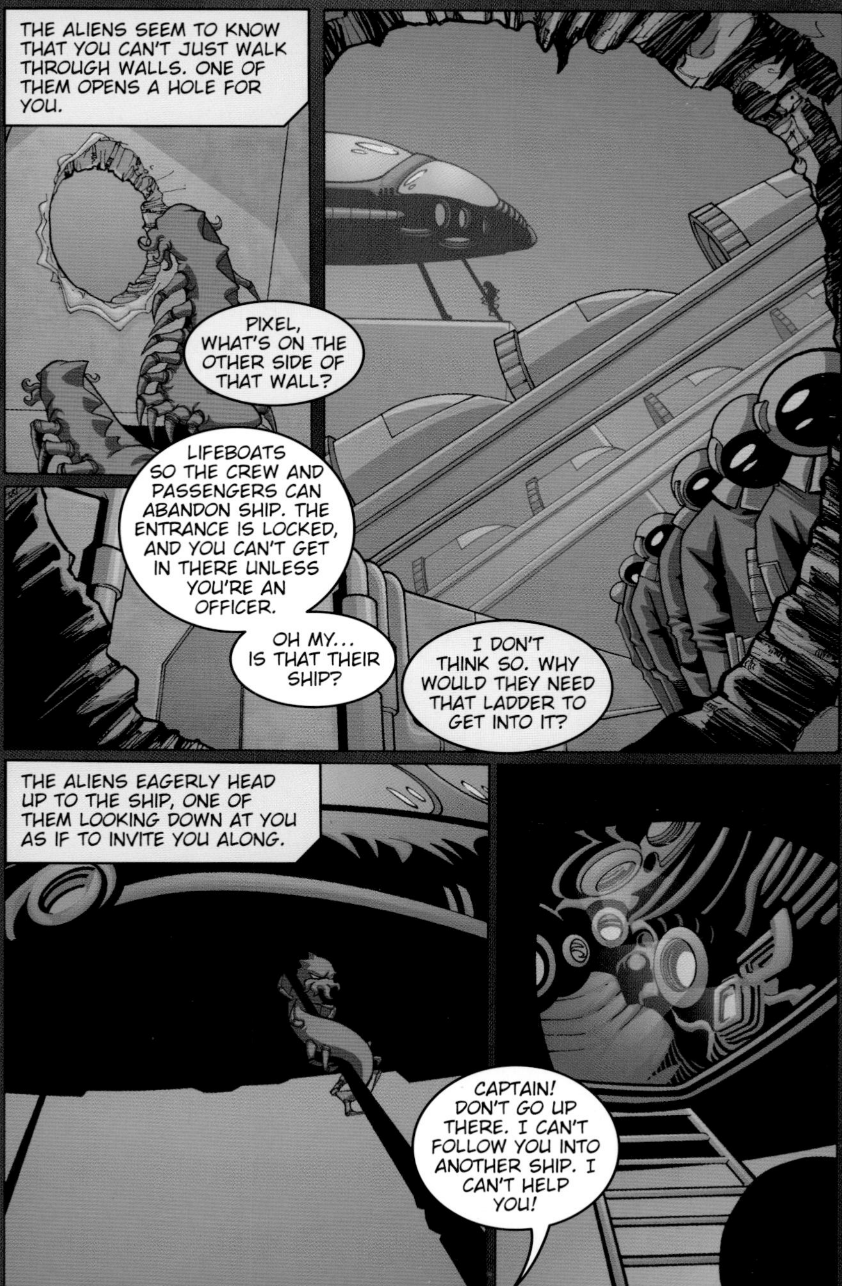
THE ALIENS SEEM TO KNOW THAT YOU CAN'T JUST WALK THROUGH WALLS. ONE OF THEM OPENS A HOLE FOR YOU.
PIXEL, WHAT'S ON THE OTHER SIDE OF THAT WALL?
LIFEBOATS SO THE CREW AND PASSENGERS CAN ABANDON SHIP. THE ENTRANCE IS LOCKED, AND YOU CAN'T GET IN THERE UNLESS YOU'RE AN OFFICER.
OH MY... IS THAT THEIR SHIP?
I DON'T THINK SO. WHY WOULD THEY NEED THAT LADDER TO GET INTO IT?
THE ALIENS EAGERLY HEAD UP TO THE SHIP, ONE OF THEM LOOKING DOWN AT YOU AS IF TO INVITE YOU ALONG.
CAPTAIN! DON'T GO UP THERE. I CAN'T FOLLOW YOU INTO ANOTHER SHIP. I CAN'T HELP YOU!

GO ON TO THE NEXT PAGE.

You're curious about this opportunity,
but it *is* an alien ship.

WILL YOU . . .

. . . play it safe and stay with Pixel?
TURN TO PAGE 30.

. . . climb up and take a look inside?
TURN TO PAGE 78.

"No, I'm sorry," you say to the alien. "I can't leave. My ship's in too much trouble. We're right on the edge of a black hole."

"Yes," the alien agrees. "Your ship was elsewhere when I came aboard. Someone connected your instruments to mine and used my ship's skip technology to transport us here. This isn't where you want to be?"

"No," you say. An idea comes to mind. "Could you take us back home?"

"I'm still connected to your computer," it says. "Let me see where your home is . . . ah-HA! I've got it!"

Before you can stop it, the alien is turning a knob and pushing buttons.

A bell tone starts to ring, and maps appear. You don't feel the jump, but your stomach turns upside down, and you suspect that you've just been transported somewhere else.

"There," the Spider Alien says, pleased. "You're back home, and we'll be going now."

GO ON TO THE NEXT PAGE.

"Um, thanks." You head down the ladder. Fido is barking like crazy. As you reach him, the alien ship floats upward and vanishes.

But where did the Spider Alien transport your ship? To Cygnus 7?

The landing bay has an opening for ships to enter and exit. It's protected by an invisible magnetic field. You look through the field.

There's a planet below the ship. It's Earth! Home, indeed.

"The captain's awake," Pixel tells you. The hologram is back to its old self. "I told her what's happening. She's on the bridge trying to slow us down."

"Slow us down?" you echo.

"Our orbit is decaying. We're spinning down toward the planet. The captain is repairing the damage done to me as fast as she can. Our saboteur, seeing that the situation has changed, has returned to me all the information I need to wake everyone up. But we still need your help. We have to abandon ship."

GO ON TO THE NEXT PAGE.

THERE'S NO TIME TO WAKE THE PASSENGERS FULLY. THEY'RE STILL HALF-ASLEEP AS YOU PACK THEM INTO ESCAPE PODS.

WHAT ABOUT PIXEL?

THE SHIP WILL BURN UP IN REENTRY SO THAT NO DANGEROUS DEBRIS LANDS ON EARTH.

WHAT? BUT PIXEL--

DON'T WORRY. I'LL FIND A WAY TO STAY WITH YOU.

EVERYONE IS FINALLY SOARING DOWN TO EARTH. YOU, ESME, AND FIDO ARE ABOUT TO BOARD THE LAST POD WHEN...

OH, NO! THIS ONE IS BROKEN. WE CAN'T USE IT.

YOU CAN'T STAY ABOARD.

I KNOW, BUT THERE'S NO OTHER WAY OFF.

YES, THERE IS! WE CAN DIVE OFF.

OF COURSE! SUIT UP!

IT MAY SOUND CRAZY, BUT WITH THE RIGHT TYPE OF SPACE SUITS, YOU CAN SPACE DIVE TO EARTH.

YOU FIND SOMETHING FOR FIDO, AND THEN THE THREE OF YOU JUMP RIGHT OUT OF THE SHIP.

TURN TO PAGE 10.

You've never used a beamer on anyone.

WILL YOU . . .

. . . try to talk to Nyche?
TURN TO PAGE 83.

. . . fire on Nyche?
TURN TO PAGE 75.

You get the beamer out of your back pocket and fire. Red-hot plasma shoots out and burns the cactus monster near the middle. Its needle-encrusted limbs flail about. You shoot again, burning more of it.

Pixel opens the door, and you make a dash for it.

Just as you're about to dive through the open door, a limb sweeps down. Cactus needles catch your clothing.

"Captain!" you hear Pixel cry, but it's too late.

Hooked on the spikes, you're lifted into the air. You see that monstrous mouth opening wide.

You are eaten by the hungry cactus monster.

THE END

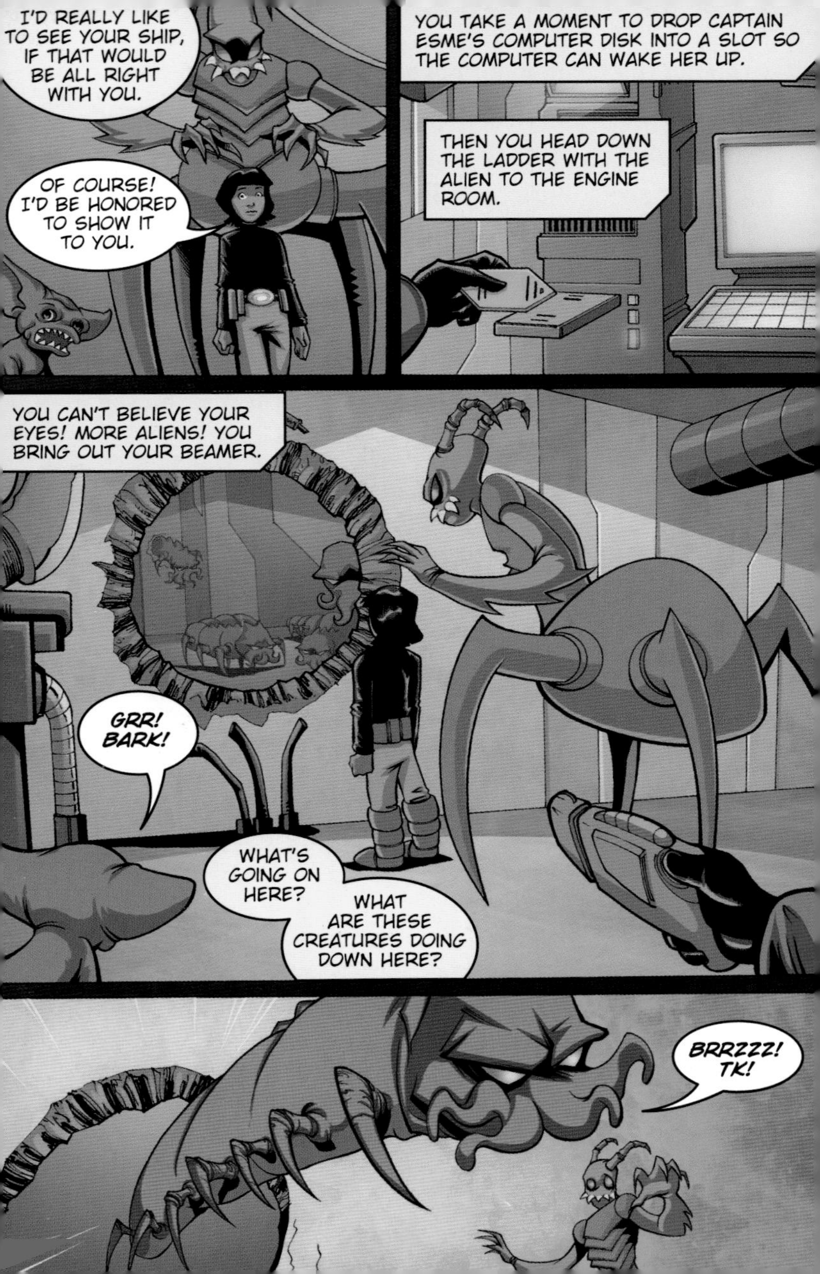
I'D REALLY LIKE TO SEE YOUR SHIP, IF THAT WOULD BE ALL RIGHT WITH YOU.
OF COURSE! I'D BE HONORED TO SHOW IT TO YOU.
YOU TAKE A MOMENT TO DROP CAPTAIN ESME'S COMPUTER DISK INTO A SLOT SO THE COMPUTER CAN WAKE HER UP.
THEN YOU HEAD DOWN THE LADDER WITH THE ALIEN TO THE ENGINE ROOM.
YOU CAN'T BELIEVE YOUR EYES! MORE ALIENS! YOU BRING OUT YOUR BEAMER.
GRR! BARK!
WHAT'S GOING ON HERE?
WHAT ARE THESE CREATURES DOING DOWN HERE?
BRRZZZ! TK!

You fire!

The shot hits Nyche square on, throwing him back into the control panel. His weapon goes flying.

"I'm sorry I had to do that," you say. Officer Nyche isn't looking your way, however. He's reaching for a button. Then he collapses over the control panel.

Alarms start to go off, and lights flash.

What's going on? You race for the vacuum tube and up to the bridge.

GO ON TO THE NEXT PAGE.

"Captain!" You arrive on the bridge, "What's happening?"

Captain Esme is entering information into the computer, glancing up at the central monitor. You see that the ship is within range of a massive, reddish white star.

"Officer Nyche just used the alien technology to jump our ship again," Esme says, "I don't know if he meant to jump us here or made a mistake, but we're next to a star about to go supernova."

A supernova! That means the star is about to collapse, sending out a huge explosion of radiation as it does so.

"Can we get away?"

"I can get us the power," the captain says, "but I'll need you to pilot."

You drop into the pilot's seat.

"You'll need to pick a planet to swing around, like a slingshot, so we have enough speed to get out in time."

You hesitate. "Did you fix the computer?"

The captain meets your eyes. "Not entirely."

GO ON TO THE NEXT PAGE.

WILL YOU . . .

. . . ask Pixel to do the calculations?
TURN TO PAGE 45.

. . . do them yourself because the computer might still be broken?
TURN TO PAGE 14.

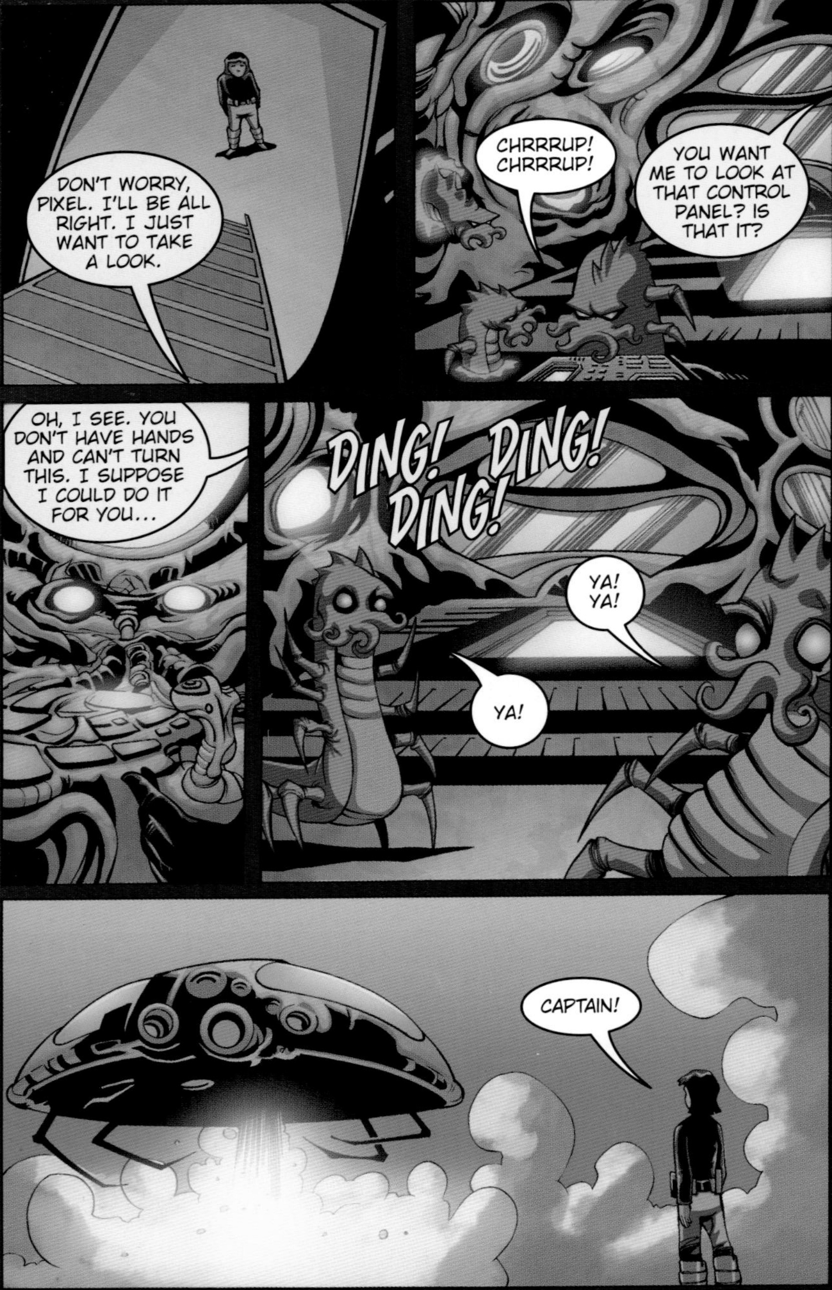
DON'T WORRY, PIXEL. I'LL BE ALL RIGHT. I JUST WANT TO TAKE A LOOK.
CHRRRUP! CHRRRUP!
YOU WANT ME TO LOOK AT THAT CONTROL PANEL? IS THAT IT?
OH, I SEE. YOU DON'T HAVE HANDS AND CAN'T TURN THIS. I SUPPOSE I COULD DO IT FOR YOU...
DING! DING! DING!
YA! YA!
YA!
CAPTAIN!

GO ON TO THE NEXT PAGE.

The monitors show a watery alien landscape. Somehow, this alien ship skipped light-years of distance and transported you to a planet far away.

The aliens phase out through the sides of the ship. The exit in the floor opens, letting in misty air that smells like ocean spray.

Cautiously, you creep down the ladder.

Your fellow passengers are being greeted by other aliens like themselves. They welcome you too.

You try to start up the alien ship again, hoping to go back, but its engines stay dead. Eventually, you learn to communicate, kind of, with the aliens. You learn that they were hitchhikers given a lift by the owner of the ship. He decided to investigate your ship but was gone so long that his friends feared he was dead. They thought they were stranded. They're grateful to you for getting them home.

Together you have many adventures. You learn to enjoy your life on this strange planet as an alien among aliens.

THE END

You reach back and pull out your beamer . . . but then hesitate.

"Pixel," you ask, "what is that?"

"It's not a mutation, Captain," Pixel says. "It's nothing from Earth."

You're shocked. "It's an alien? How did it get on the ship? How did it get in here?"

"I don't know."

One thing is clear, the cactus creature has been keeping this alien trapped in the arboretum. With the cactus creature gone, the alien can leave. It looks fast. If you open the door, it will probably get out.

You can't just let it wander about the ship. Who knows what damage it might do?

The alien hasn't attacked. It's watching you, waiting to see what you will do. Fido snarls and stands before you protectively.

GO ON TO THE NEXT PAGE.

You have to do something.
WILL YOU . . .

. . . try to talk to it?
TURN TO PAGE 94.

. . . sic Fido on it?
TURN TO PAGE 90.

The ship is flying off!

WILL YOU . . .

. . . aim for the bottom of it and shoot?
TURN TO PAGE 34.

. . . aim for the top of it and shoot?
TURN TO PAGE 98.

"Officer Nyche, this is wrong." You try to sway him.

"Maybe," he says, "but so long as I have this amazing alien technology, I refuse to give up control of this ship or let anyone stop me. Not even you."

Unexpectedly, he pulls the trigger! The light from his plasma gun is hot and blinding, but you feel no pain. The last thing you see is Officer Nyche's look of regret as you tumble to the floor.

"I didn't bother to upload your information to disk," you hear his voice say. And the last thing you hear is, "I thought you were just a kid and no danger to me. Looks like I was wrong."

THE END

"Oh no!" Officer Nyche croaks. "The cactus was keeping the alien in the arboretum."

"Alien?"

"If you distracted the cactus—"

"There's an alien lose on the ship?" Officer Arion snaps angrily.

"It will head to its ship in the docking bay," Nyche says.

"What will it do if it gets to it?"

"Strand us here." Nyche's voice trembles. "That ship can jump across light-years. I used it to get us here to the black hole. Without it, we're stuck."

"I'll stop the alien." Arion locks thick magnetic cuffs on Nyche's wrists and attaches the cuffs to the wall. "Stay here with the prisoner," he orders Pixel.

"Come on," the security officer commands you. The two of you race down the corridor to the elevators.

GO ON TO THE NEXT PAGE.

The elevator. Pixel warned you about the elevator.

WILL YOU . . .

. . . let Officer Arion handle the problem?
TURN TO PAGE 102.

. . . yell at Officer Arion not to use the elevator?
TURN TO PAGE 107.

"Yes," you say, "I'd love to be part of your crew and journey across the universe with you."

After all, you think, *if this ship can really jump around the universe, then I can always visit Earth or Cygnus 7, right?*

The Spider Alien is delighted, as are his hitchhiking friends. The alien touches buttons. The ladder in the floor pulls up. You hear Fido still barking as the opening in the floor closes. You feel a wobble as the alien ship starts to float, its legs folding up.

Star maps in swirling colors appear on the monitors, as well as a three-dimensional image of the galaxy spinning overhead.

"Hm," says the Spider Alien. "There, I think." It points to a particular spot. "There's an amazing star nursery there."

A STAR NURSERY! YOU REMEMBER HEARING ABOUT THOSE FROM YOUR ASTRONOMY CLASS.

IN A BLINK, YOU'RE THERE. GAZING OUT AT GIANT GAS CLOUDS...

ALONG WITH YOUR ALIEN FRIENDS, YOU SEE FIRSTHAND HOW THOSE GASES COMPRESS INTO HYDROGEN AND HELIUM.

THE TEMPERATURE IN THAT BALL OF GASES GOES UP TO 15,000,000 DEGREES!

ATOMIC PARTICLES MOVE VERY FAST AT THAT TEMPERATURE, SENDING OUT ENERGY AND LIGHT...

THIS IS AWESOME!

IT'S THE MOST AMAZING THING YOU'VE EVER SEEN... AND IT'S ONLY THE BEGINNING.

TURN TO PAGE 61.

The choice is yours. The future is in your hands.

THE END

AI-EEEEEE!

YOU FIRE AT ANOTHER!

WATCH OUT! IF IT TOUCHES YOU--

THE ALIEN KNOCKS RIGHT INTO YOU, AND YOU BEGIN TO FEEL AN ODD SENSATION...

...AS THE ATOMS OF YOUR BODY START TO BREAK APART...

...UNTIL THERE'S NOTHING LEFT.

THE END

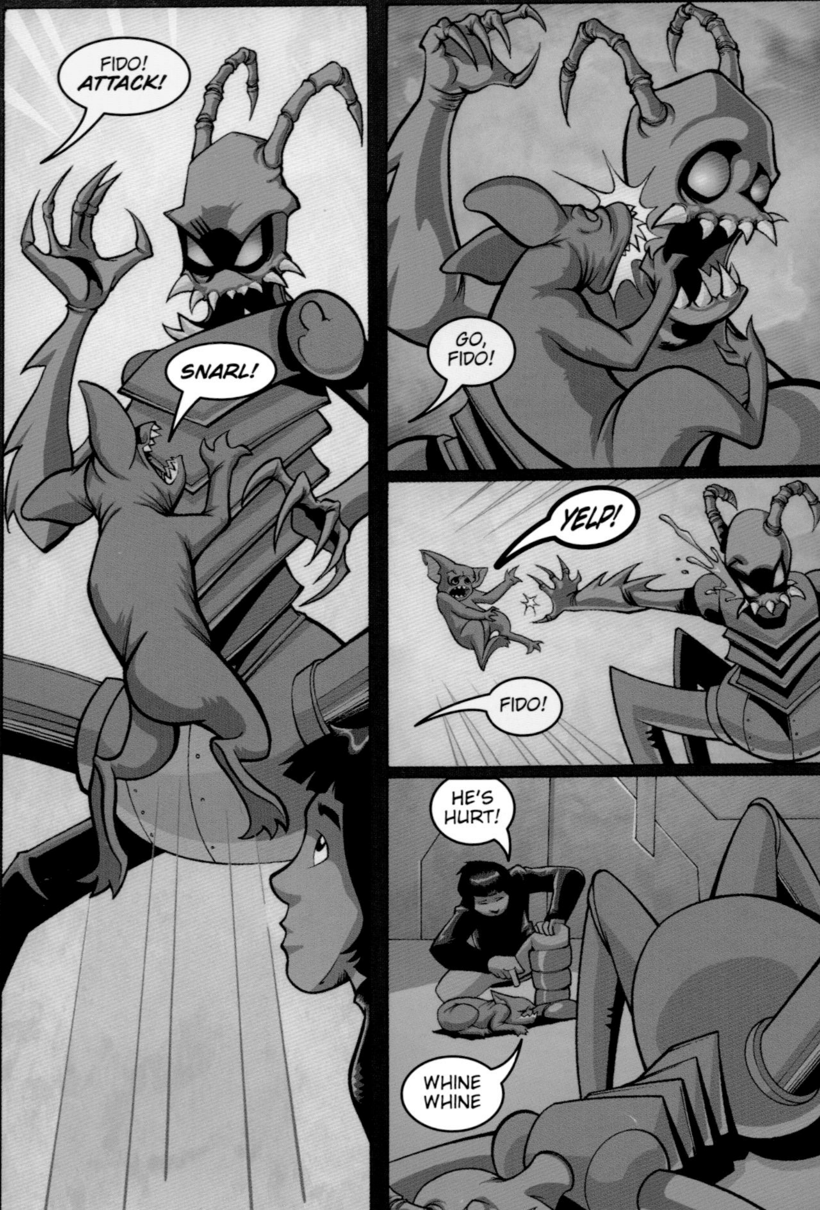
FIDO! ATTACK!
SNARL!
GO, FIDO!
YELP!
FIDO!
HE'S HURT!
WHINE WHINE

GO ON TO THE NEXT PAGE.

You check to make sure the alien is dead, then scoop up Fido and take him to a first aid station. You put him gently into a healing container.

"Fido was badly hurt. He will need to stay here for a while," Pixel says, as you slip Captain Esme's disk into a slot at a computer station.

"How long will it take you to wake the captain?" you ask.

"About forty minutes."

Forty minutes? You remember seeing something moving around in the engine room. Perhaps you should use this time to check out what's going on down there.

GO ON TO THE NEXT PAGE.

It's probably better to wait.
Then again, you do have a weapon.

WILL YOU . . .

. . . head down to the engine room?
TURN TO PAGE 55.

. . . sit in the computer room and wait while
Captain Esme is woken up?
TURN TO PAGE 41.

"The alien you trapped is gone!" you shout at Nyche.

"WHAT? I don't believe it! My cactus—"

"—is destroyed. The alien is gone."

Nyche lowers the plasma gun, stunned. "Then we're stuck out here. I was using that alien's ship to jump us across light-years. Without that technology, we can't return to where we were."

This is terrible! Shocked as you are by the news, you manage to say to Nyche: "Then we'll need everyone's help to survive out here, won't we?"

You gather the disks and wake everyone. The ship becomes your home. Pixel, who picked up some information about the alien while connected to it, works with Nyche. Together they teach you about alien biology and alien thought and speech. This becomes useful as the ship starts to encounter other spacefaring races. You become a true xenobiologist, an expert in all things alien. Thanks to you, the ship becomes an international meeting place for many species, a United Nations in space.

THE END

"Fido, back. Sit!" you command. Fido, with a final growl, reluctantly obeys.

You hold up empty hands, your heart pounding in fear, but the alien never moves.

"Someone trapped you here," you say to it in a calm, even voice. "Who did that to you and why? And how did you come to be on my ship?"

The alien tilts its head, as if your attempt to communicate interests it.

"I'm not sure it can talk to you," Pixel ventures. "Even if it knows how to use words, it doesn't have a human mouth or vocal cords."

You feel a little foolish for not realizing that. Pixel's comment, however, has gotten the alien's attention. Slowly, as if to show it means no harm, it reaches out its long limbs to touch Pixel.

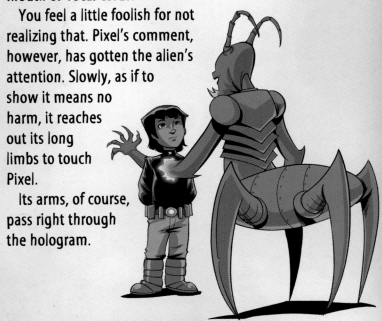

Its arms, of course, pass right through the hologram.

GO ON TO THE NEXT PAGE.

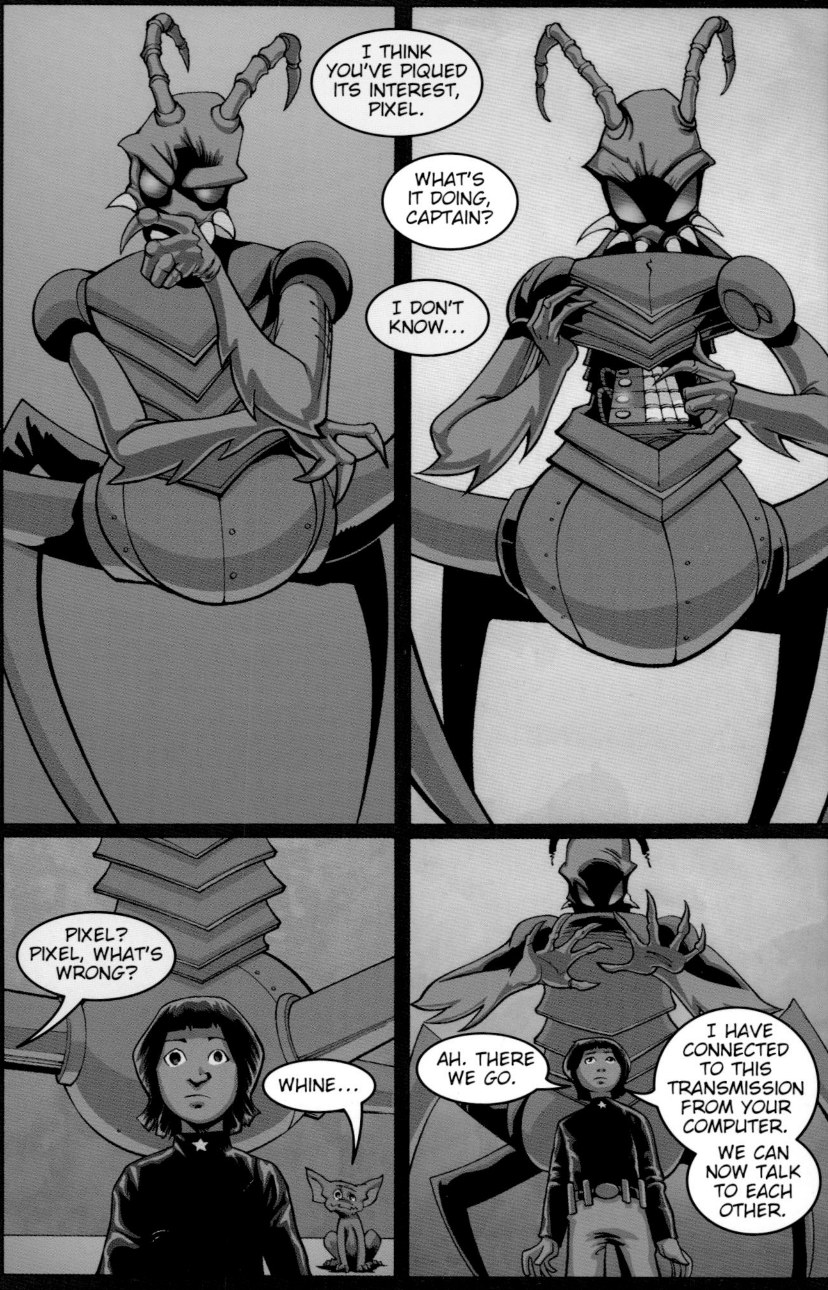
I THINK YOU'VE PIQUED ITS INTEREST, PIXEL.
WHAT'S IT DOING, CAPTAIN?
I DON'T KNOW...
PIXEL? PIXEL, WHAT'S WRONG?
WHINE...
AH. THERE WE GO.
I HAVE CONNECTED TO THIS TRANSMISSION FROM YOUR COMPUTER.
WE CAN NOW TALK TO EACH OTHER.

GO ON TO THE NEXT PAGE.

You realize that the alien has found a way to talk through Pixel!

"What are you, and how did you get aboard this ship?" you ask.

"I am a traveler," the hologram explains for the alien. "My ship picked up a signal from your ship, and I came aboard in curiosity. I am always looking to find and understand new species."

The alien dips its head as if to apologize. "I fear I did something very wrong, because the one who greeted me knocked me out and imprisoned me here. I've been very scared," the alien adds. "I thought you meant to eat me."

"Eat you!" You gasp in horror. "We wouldn't do that."

The hologram sighs with relief. "Thank you! I'm really very sorry if I trespassed. If you'll allow me to return to my ship, I'll leave and never bother you again."

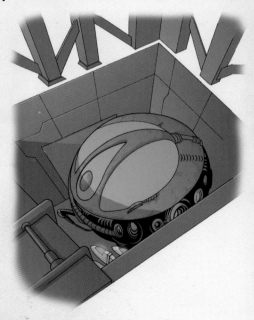

GO ON TO THE NEXT PAGE.

You feel bad for the friendly alien, but there are a lot of unanswered questions.

WILL YOU . . .

. . . let the alien go? You have to get the captain back.
TURN TO PAGE 47.

. . . ask to see its ship?
TURN TO PAGE 74.

. . . ask the alien if it will stay awhile?
TURN TO PAGE 43.

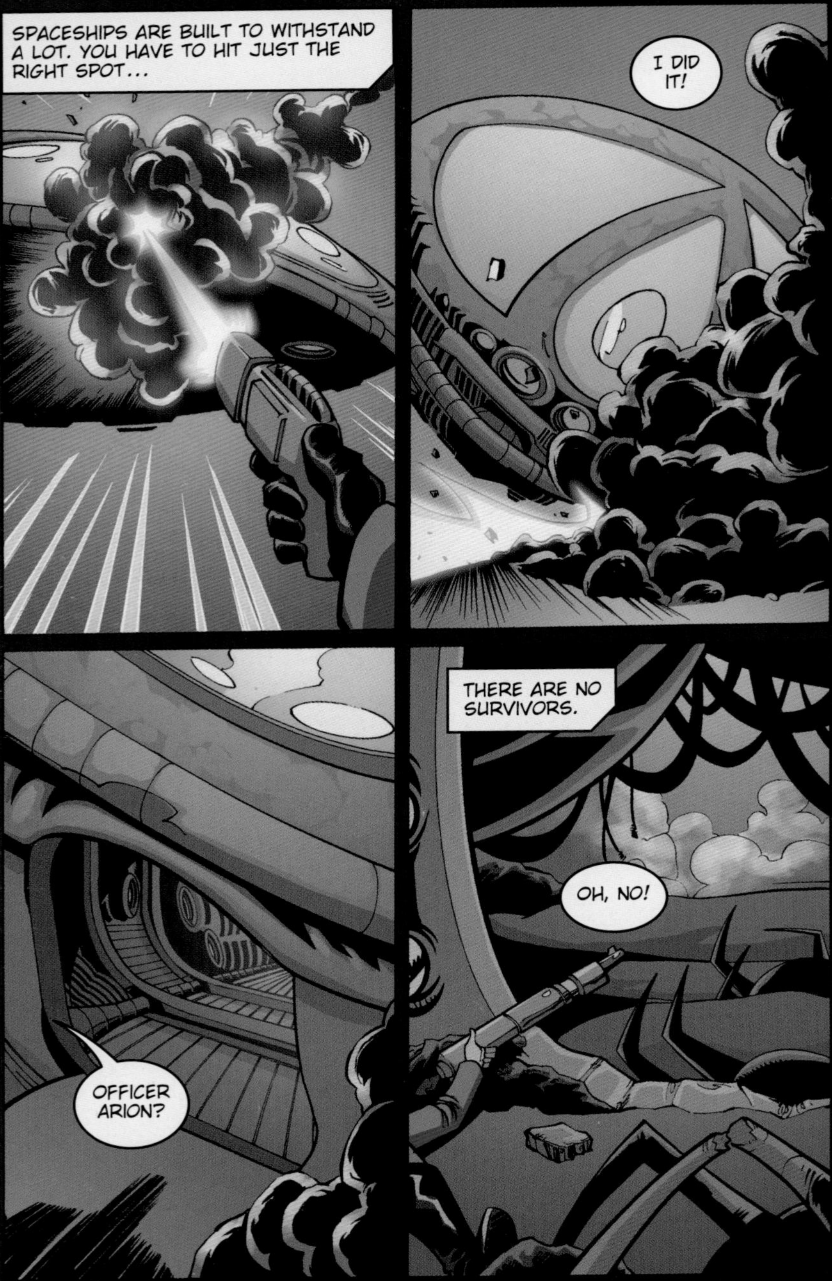
SPACESHIPS ARE BUILT TO WITHSTAND A LOT. YOU HAVE TO HIT JUST THE RIGHT SPOT...
I DID IT!
OFFICER ARION?
THERE ARE NO SURVIVORS.
OH, NO!

GO ON TO THE NEXT PAGE.

You head back to the storage room.

"Did you stop it?" Pixel asks.

"I brought down the ship," you admit sadly. "But Officer Arion and the alien were crushed inside."

"What?" Officer Nyche cries out in horror. "If the alien is gone, then there's no way for us to jump across light-years, especially if the ship's been destroyed too."

"The ship wasn't completely destroyed," you protest. "Only the top was flattened."

Nyche looks hopeful. "Maybe the engine wasn't damaged, then."

You take the disks and wake the rest of the people. Captain Esme is understanding. She knows you did what you had to do.

The ship becomes your permanent home. You and Nyche both join up with the ship's engineers to study the alien vessel. You grow up to be the chief engineer. Although you never quite figure out how to jump over light-years, your innovations allow your ship to travel farther and faster than you ever had dreamed, across this new and unexplored area of space.

THE END

The Cryo Level stores more than just passengers. All the stuff people brought from Earth and all the things they might need on another planet are on that level. You creep down the corridors until you come to the storeroom. You wait. It isn't long before you hear a door open. You see the man head out.

Quick as you can, you dart in. It is dim, almost dark in there. Up ahead are the disks. A lot of them are high up and out of reach. Maybe if you stand on the chair?

You start to climb up . . . then you freeze.

Footsteps! The saboteur is already on his way back! There are two disks low enough to grab. The one to the right reads "SECURITY OFFICER," and the one to the left reads, "CAPTAIN."

You hear the door sliding open. You see the man's shadow . . .

You only have time to grab one disk and escape.

WILL YOU . . .

. . . grab the security officer's disk and dive
through the right cargo hatch?
TURN TO PAGE 104.

. . . grab the captain's disk and dive
through the left hatch?
TURN TO PAGE 42.

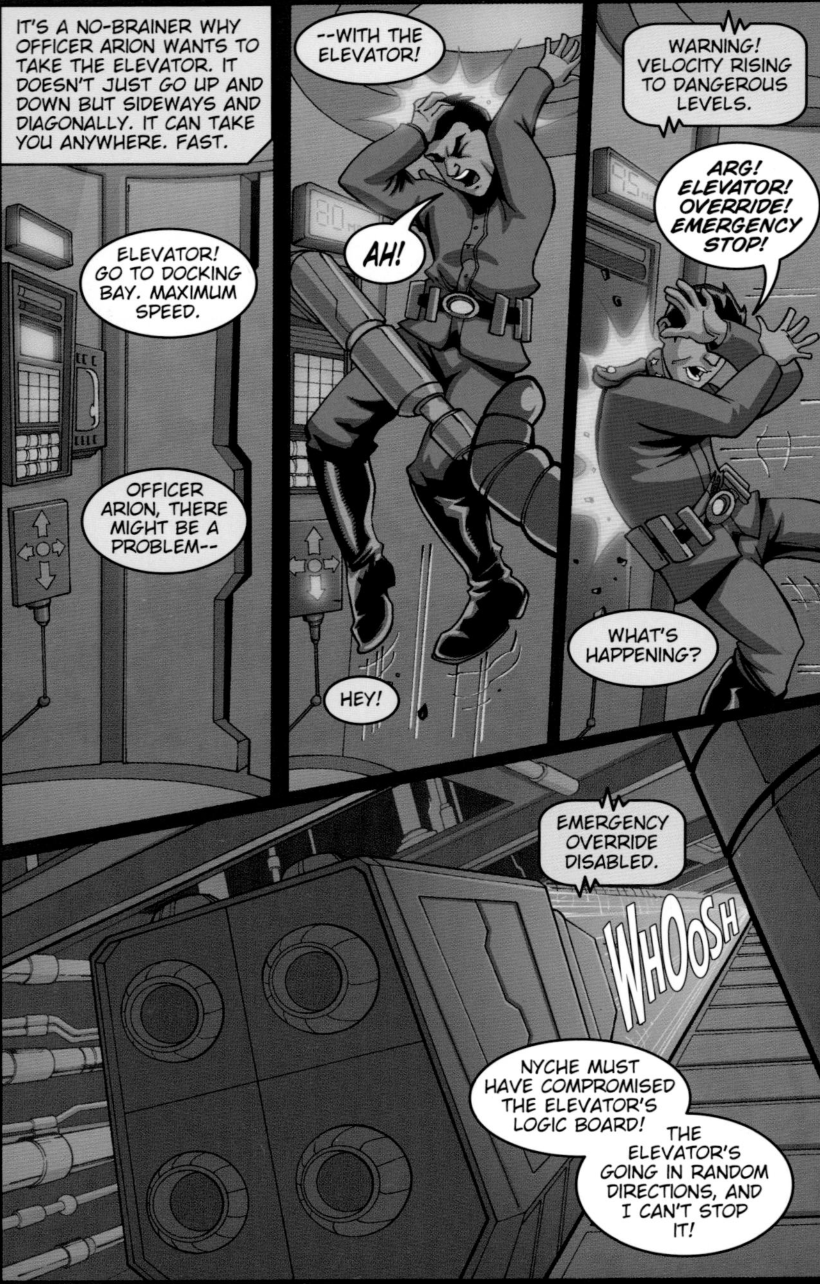
IT'S A NO-BRAINER WHY OFFICER ARION WANTS TO TAKE THE ELEVATOR. IT DOESN'T JUST GO UP AND DOWN BUT SIDEWAYS AND DIAGONALLY. IT CAN TAKE YOU ANYWHERE. FAST.
ELEVATOR! GO TO DOCKING BAY. MAXIMUM SPEED.
OFFICER ARION, THERE MIGHT BE A PROBLEM--
--WITH THE ELEVATOR!
AH!
HEY!
WARNING! VELOCITY RISING TO DANGEROUS LEVELS.
ARG! ELEVATOR! OVERRIDE! EMERGENCY STOP!
WHAT'S HAPPENING?
EMERGENCY OVERRIDE DISABLED.
WHOOSH
NYCHE MUST HAVE COMPROMISED THE ELEVATOR'S LOGIC BOARD!
THE ELEVATOR'S GOING IN RANDOM DIRECTIONS, AND I CAN'T STOP IT!

GO ON TO THE NEXT PAGE.

The elevator speeds up even faster. Officer Arion looks at you. He doesn't have to say anything. You know what's about to happen. You learned it in class before the ship left Earth.

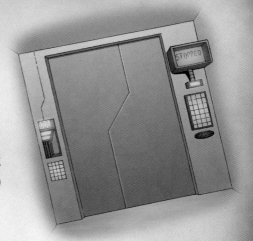

It's all about kinetic energy. If you tumble down a hill, you'll keep tumbling for a little while longer even after you've reached the bottom because your mass and the speed you were going at create extra *kinetic energy,* the energy that keeps you moving.

This is the formula for the amount of kinetic energy you will have when the elevator stops: one-half *m*, times *v*, times *v*, equals *Ek*.

$$\tfrac{1}{2}mv^2 = Ek$$

m is your mass.

v is the velocity of the elevator.

Ek is the kinetic energy you have.

This means when the elevator reaches the end of the elevator shaft . . . you and Officer Arion will keep going.

I should have listened to Pixel, you think, even as the elevator slams to a stop and you smash into the elevator wall.

THE END

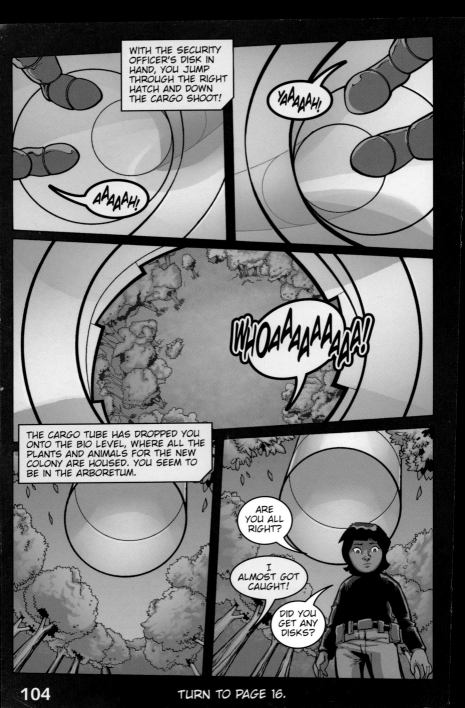

WITH THE SECURITY OFFICER'S DISK IN HAND, YOU JUMP THROUGH THE RIGHT HATCH AND DOWN THE CARGO SHOOT!

YAAAAH!

AAAAAH!

WHOAAAAAAAAA!

THE CARGO TUBE HAS DROPPED YOU ONTO THE BIO LEVEL, WHERE ALL THE PLANTS AND ANIMALS FOR THE NEW COLONY ARE HOUSED. YOU SEEM TO BE IN THE ARBORETUM.

ARE YOU ALL RIGHT?

I ALMOST GOT CAUGHT!

DID YOU GET ANY DISKS?

TURN TO PAGE 16.

You get the beamer out of your back pocket. You don't want to hurt the dog, just scare it away, so you fire at its feet. Red-hot plasma shoots out. You hit the dog's toes. It yelps and jumps aside.

You make a dive through the door. Even as you do, however, you hear an angry snarl. From the corner of your eye, you see the creature leaping. Its needle-sharp teeth latch onto your neck!

"Captain!" you hear Pixel cry, but it's too late. Within a few heartbeats, the mutated mutt has made a meal of you.

THE END

After Officer Nyche is locked up and the information on the disks are back in Pixel's memory banks, you head up to the bridge.

Captain Esme and the alien are waiting. "Everything is set up for the jump," she says. "Given all you've done, we thought you should push the button."

She points to it, and you—a bit nervous, a bit excited—reach for it. "Now?" you ask.

Captain Esme and the alien both nod.

You push the button. There is a flicker as if the whole universe has blinked, as the image on the screen changes.

The black hole is gone. In its place is a beautiful blue and green planet, almost as pretty as Earth. A yellow sun glows in the distance.

Cygnus 7.

TURN TO PAGE 21.

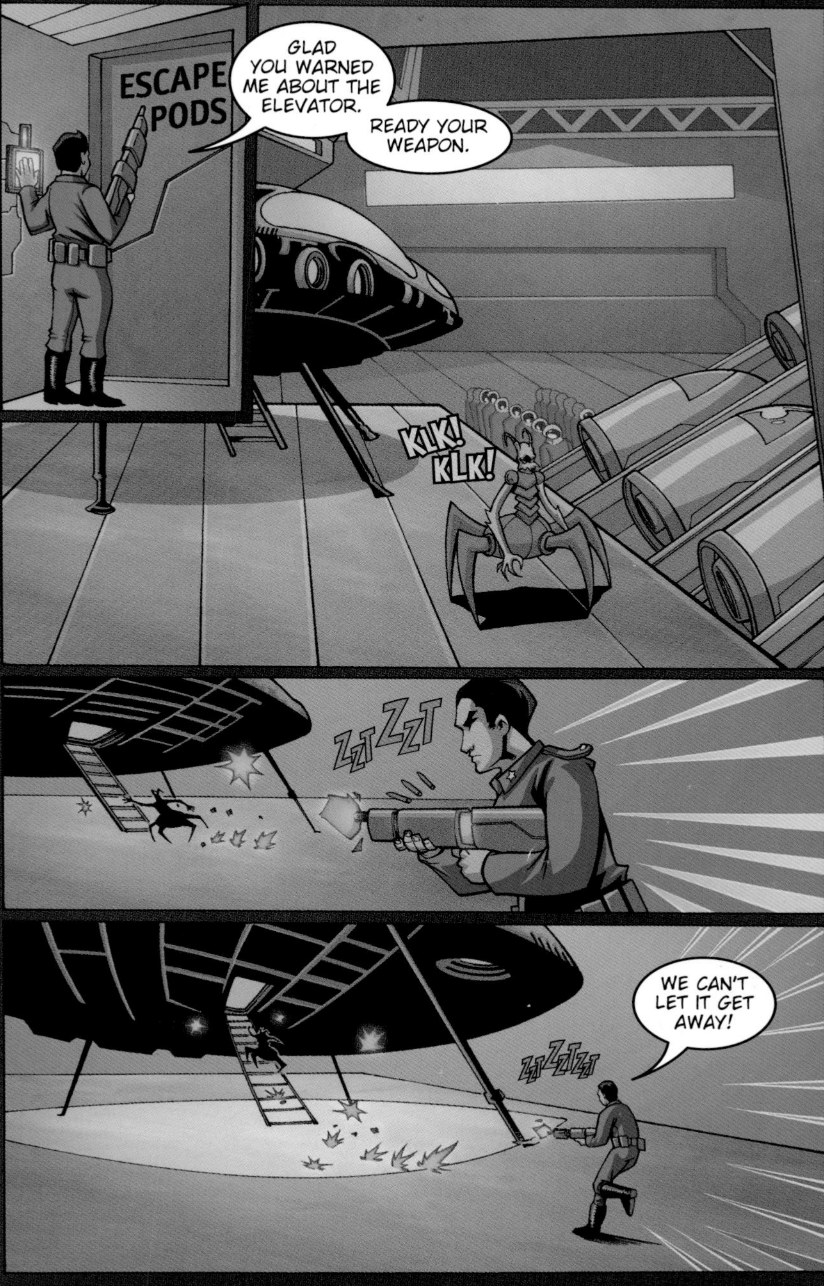
ESCAPE PODS
GLAD YOU WARNED ME ABOUT THE ELEVATOR.
READY YOUR WEAPON.
KLK! KLK!
ZZT ZZT
WE CAN'T LET IT GET AWAY!

GO ON TO THE NEXT PAGE.

That's one scary creature!

WILL YOU . . .

. . . shoot at the alien?
TURN TO PAGE 110.

. . . hold back and see what happens?
TURN TO PAGE 19.

You land unharmed. Emergency crews from Mission Command base arrive to meet you and see if you're all right. Soon your story is known around the world. Everyone wants to talk to you and learn about the alien. There are media appearances, and you're even given a medal for your heroic deeds. You saved everyone on board that ship.

As a special gift, you're given a computer with many terabytes of memory. Turning it on, you see a familiar face and hear a familiar voice.

"I told you I'd find a way to be with you, my friend," says Pixel. You get to keep your faithful dog Fido as well.

You don't know if your family will try again to travel to Cygnus 7. For now, you're just happy to be back on Earth, your adventures in space over, and everyone you care about safe and sound.

THE END

The alien is almost up the ladder. You shoot! Bug juice splatters all over.

Gross!

The bug bits fall off the ladder and to the floor. They twitch and shudder before going still.

"Good shooting!" Officer Arion compliments you, catching his breath.

But even as you're celebrating, the alien ship comes to life. The ladder folds up. The ship hums and rises. Its legs fold up. And then . . . it vanishes!

Mystified, the two of you head back to the storage room to Pixel and Nyche.

"Did you stop the alien?" Pixel asks.

"We blew it up," you say. "But then the ship vanished."

"Oh, no!" Officer Nyche cries out in horror. "The alien was biologically connected to that ship. That's why the ship disappeared from this dimension after you destroyed it."

"So the ship is gone. What does that mean?" Officer Arion asks.

"It means we have no way to get back to any area of space we know," says Nyche.

You gather all the disks and wake everyone up. Captain Esme, after hearing the whole story, is understanding. "You did the best you knew how to do," she says.

"But what are we going to do now?" you ask. "Where are we going to live?"

GO ON TO THE NEXT PAGE.

Where indeed?

On the ship itself, as it turns out. It becomes your permanent home. Officer Nyche, regretting what he did, works hard to create new plants and animals to keep everyone well fed and healthy. He also studies what's left of the alien. You're interested in the alien too—since unfortunately you were the one who zapped it—and soon Nyche is letting you help him. He teaches you all he knows.

You become a biologist, growing and creating all kinds of new species on your soaring laboratory in space and learning all about life on alien worlds.

THE END

EXPERIENCE ALL OF THE TWISTED JOURNEYS®